Jessica —

May your life be mythical!

Natasha

Chosen of the Gods
Hammerfall

Natasha Cover

Sunday

Do you ever dream that you're running, and you don't know what from, or where to – all you know is that you just can't run fast enough? Yeah. I have that dream a lot.

Liam ran up the hill, his breath catching in his chest as his legs burned with the fiery ache of the slope. It had been a long day, first with the car chase and now this. The perp had ditched his car in the middle of the road and hit the ground running, and Liam had needed to radio in backup from his bike before he could begin the pursuit on foot. Now they were nearing the caves, and he could only hope that his superiors had managed to clear out the civilians.

He rounded a bend and came through the trees into a horse track. No one was around, and Liam took a moment to praise God for that as he ran. Just barely in sight was his target, rounding yet another corner and heading for the entrance to the caverns. Liam took a deep breath and pushed himself on, one hand on his holster to keep his gun in place, though he prayed he wouldn't have to use it.

It was an unnaturally cold day, which made his exertion that much more difficult. Tucson should never be in the 50's during the day, much less in the middle of summer. The scientists put it down to global warming, and people went along with it – but no one talked about the fact that the cold had come suddenly, the weather dropping from the mid-90's to 60° within hours. The change had come just a few days ago, and it wasn't just in Arizona. The whole world's weather was strangely cold.

Liam shook his head, struggling to clear his thoughts as his feet left the hard packed dirt road and pounded instead on the rough stone of the cavern. His footsteps and ragged breathing echoed eerily as he rounded the bends, slowing slightly as he remembered the drops he had seen as a child. It had been years since he had visited Colossal Cave, but the memory of it still haunted him – the ever-present darkness, the unreal way that sound carried, and the seemingly bottomless holes that threatened to swallow you up if you lost your footing.

The memory of it shook him, and Liam drew his gun, more an act of familiarity and comfort than out of any intent to use it. No sooner had he done so than his target stepped out in front of him, swinging a crowbar.

Liam ducked and continued forward, his momentum working for him as he swung his pistol and smacked the butt into the man's kneecap. The man went down with a mangled shriek and Liam followed him, grappling for the crowbar. They tussled for a moment, but Liam was stronger and his opponent was blinded by tears of pain. Liam wrenched the bar away and threw it to the side, hearing it clang against the floor.

The thief's shrieks grew more coherent as he lunged for Liam, fingers raking at his face. The cop blocked him, struggling to retain the upper hand. He grimaced at a sharp pain as blood was drawn on his cheek and smacked aside grasping fingers, grabbing the man's wrist. Liam suddenly dropped his weight, landing heavily on his mark's chest, and nodded in satisfaction at his sudden expulsion of air.

Liam reached behind him, making use of what little time his move had bought him to grab his handcuffs from his belt. He snapped one cuff around the man's wrist and dove for the other, but his opponent had the strength of desperation on his side and rolled – sending them both over the edge of a dark pit.

The frost was creeping in…

The first thing Liam noticed when he awoke was the cold, pressing in on him through his jacket as he lay upon the chilled, hard floor. His body ached, and he groaned as he opened his eyes. That was when he noticed the darkness that cloaked his surroundings. Whereas the area where he and the crook had tussled retained some lighting from the entrance of the cave, here there was none. With a grimace he sat up and pulled out his flashlight, twisting the head to turn it on.

Light flooded his surroundings, and Liam blinked to clear his vision. It took a minute before he could see, and when he could he was amazed to be alive. Several stalagmites surrounded him, and it was a miracle that neither he nor the man he'd chased had landed on one. Liam rolled over and stood unsteadily, grunting. His mark lay near him, still unconscious, and Liam swiftly cuffed his other arm behind his back.

That task done, the cop looked up. They had fallen a good twenty or thirty feet, and he could see no easy way out – particularly not with the frost beginning to build up on the walls of the cave. Liam shivered as he touched the wall, his breath fogging in the air. From the temperature he thought they'd been out of it for a few hours – it had been midday when he'd begun the car chase, and judging from the last few days, the weather should only have dropped this low in the evening.

But no, he thought, that didn't make sense. He'd called in backup, and if they'd been out of it for hours, surely his support would have come in. Perhaps they'd come and passed him by, but he didn't think that was likely. Maybe the cold was just…colder, here in the cave. Liam rubbed the rising bump on his head, hoping that he was thinking clearly.

After a moment he reached for his radio to check in, but found it broken from his fall. A groan drew his attention back to his companion, and he looked the young man over as he began to wake. The force had little information on Kevin Darwin – no previous criminal records, and too young to have fingerprints on file. They had only identified him because he had given his ID to the bank teller to deposit a check before trying to rob the place.

He looked rather the worse for wear, with his black jeans torn at the knees – one of which was already beginning to swell purple where Liam's pistol had made contact. The cop winced as Kevin opened his eyes – he hadn't realized just how young the man was. As he moaned at the brightness of Liam's flashlight the cop turned the beam away, taking an inventory of his own wounds. He had gotten away with just a few scrapes and bruises from the fall, similar to those Kevin had, and considered himself extraordinarily lucky given the length of the drop. His right cheek was sticky with blood, and Liam grimaced in distaste as he touched it. The pain, thankfully, had long since died away to a steady, dull ache.

Liam watched as the reality of the situation struck Kevin and he began to wriggle, trying to get his legs under him to stand. It wasn't easy to do in handcuffs, and Liam bit back a laugh as he watched. "Don't try it, kid," he said after a moment. "Not many places you could go even if you *could* get up." The teen looked at him resentfully and Liam shrugged, turning to take another look at their surroundings. His statement was true – there were two tunnels from where they stood, one of which ended ten feet down in a cave-in. The second tunnel was smaller and dark, and Liam found it…familiar?

"It's cold," whimpered the young man from behind him, and Liam nodded his agreement as he stepped forward. Something about the tunnel called to him, and he shivered as he laid his hand against the wall. Though he would swear he'd never been here before, Liam almost thought he recognized the place. He peered into the darkness and thought he could make out a faint blue glow.

"C'mon, kid, let's take a look around." He turned back to Kevin and hauled him to his feet, ignoring the weary moan this elicited.

"Shouldn't we wait for help?" the young man asked pitifully.

Liam shook his head, shifting to support the thief's injured leg. "I don't know how long we've been out; they might've already come and gone. But there's no harm in taking a look around while we wait." The kid groaned again, but he didn't struggle when Liam headed down the tunnel.

"Sir," he said after a moment, "You should know…the money isn't for me, there was this guy, he made me do it-"

"Save it for the judge, kid," Liam said quietly. He'd heard it before, both less and more convincingly, but the teen just didn't strike him as a criminal. The best didn't, of course, and he was certainly streetwise from the way he fought, but that didn't mark him as a danger to society – not like some of the guys Liam had caught. All the same, the kid had broken the law; his punishment wasn't for Liam to decide.

The blue light ahead grew brighter the farther they went, and finally Liam turned off his flashlight. Though dim, the light was bright enough to see by, though it added to the eerie nature of the cave. Shadows danced around them, and Liam reached again for his gun only to find it missing, tossed aside in the struggle up above.

As they rounded one last bend, the duo let out a gasp. Before them was a small rounded cavern. It gleamed with a brilliant blue light that emanated from the center of the room, where a large stalagmite that ended in a flat surface rather than a point rose from the floor, the only protrusion in the otherwise smooth room. Atop of the stalagmite lay the source of the light – a sledgehammer.

Liam stared at it as he walked Kevin to the wall, leaning him against it and helping him to slide down. The kid gave a weak smile of gratitude that Liam didn't see, too intent on the hammer.

Slowly he walked towards it, not noticing that as he did so the ground beneath his feet crackled as ice broke from his weight. Liam stretched out one hand, his mind vaguely aware that the stalagmite ended at the perfect height for him to reach. He hesitated for a moment above the handle, and as he did so he felt a slight breeze on the back of his neck as static electricity made his hair rise.

Liam...

He gripped the pommel, and everything went white – then black.

My father leans forward and whispers a single word into my brother's ear before stepping back, nodding to me through the tears he sheds.

I step forward, my hammer extended for one last task here in Asgard. Before me burns a bright fire, in the center of which lies my brother. The straw beneath him burns brightly, soon to consume him. For but a moment I close my eyes, fighting my sorrow, but then I conquer my anguish – at least temporarily – and open them once more. Mjolnir moves in my hand, etching the shape of the rune of life in the air as I bless him. Slowly I step back, my task completed as I bid Baldr his final farewell. Together I and my remaining brothers push the boat out to sea, sending my dear brother and his wife on their final voyage. Around us, a crowd of all those whose lives he has touched look on in sorrow.

My father steps up to me, laying a hand on my shoulder. With a forced smile I look at him, thinking how much white has been added to his beard by this ordeal. He meets my gaze for a moment, his single eye sharp with the knowledge of what I feel, and I am forced to glance away by the shared sorrow I see there. My father touches my cheek, bringing my eyes back to him, and I feel the weight of what he is about to say.

"It has begun." His voice is deep, his seriousness plain to see, and his words are for me alone. "The End is near. You know what you must do."

I nod, remembering our many councils on how best to prepare for this day, and grip Mjolnir a little tighter. He returns my nod and squeezes my shoulder; it is his turn to force a smile. I feel him look deeper into me, and I know that his next words are not for my benefit alone.

"And you, brave lad – you too shall have your part to play."

Liam…

"Liam awoke to the cold, a white ceiling, and the smell of medical supplies.

He lay there for a moment, confused. He distinctly remembered being in a cave and falling, and…the hammer! Of course!

Liam sat bolt upright, looking around. How had he gotten here? His brow furrowed in puzzlement as he struggled to remember. After the flash of light, there was nothing. He looked around him but saw no clues – just a private room that looked like any hospital he had ever been in, with a small TV hanging from one corner of the ceiling and no windows. He thought for a moment of Kevin and hoped he was alright – perhaps backup had arrived and found them after all.

Liam arched his back and then froze, waiting for the pain to kick in – but none seemed forthcoming. *Must be good painkillers*, he thought as he rolled his shoulders. He reached up to feel his cheek, expecting to find it bandaged, but instead found a thick stubble. *What the-!* Liam was quite sure he had shaved that morning, as the dress code of his force required a clean shaven face or a neatly trimmed beard.

So what in the world was he doing with that much hair on his face?

Liam glanced around for a mirror and instead found his gun sitting on the dresser beside his bed. He distinctly remembered having dropped it – perhaps one of his squad mates had found it. Looking down, he was surprised to find himself in his normal uniform - albeit one stained with dirt and boasting a few rips – rather than a hospital gown.

Liam leaned back, shaking his head and wishing he knew what was going on. No sooner had he done so than the TV flashed on, revealing a news reporter at what he recognized as the Colossal Cave parking lot. Several police cars were parked in it, their lights still flashing, and Liam recognized his roommate off in the distance keeping the crowd at bay. The time read a mere four hours after he had begun the chase.

Liam blinked in surprise as the chief of his department, Helen, emerged from the cave with Kevin in tow. *How did they manage to rescue me and miss him?* he wondered.

They didn't. Liam shook his head – now he was answering his own questions. For a moment he thought he heard a frustrated sigh, but he ignored it, focusing on where the camera was now zooming in on Kevin. He was almost to the police car and was decidedly agitated, speaking loudly with his escort. The volume of the television rose as Liam strained to hear, making the voices discernable.

"I'm telling you, there was this flash of light and then this angel appeared! She grabbed the cop and flew out, they just disappeared, man! I-"

He was cut off as Helen shoved him into the car and closed the door, gesturing for her officers to fall in. The camera panned back to the reporter and the TV flicked off as Liam gaped at it. Taken by an angel? Did that make this the afterlife?

He shivered, suddenly unnerved. No version of heaven he'd ever heard of had contained a hospital.

A creak outside of the door made him glance over, his hand reaching for his sidearm. Liam waited for a moment, but all was still, with only the fog of his breath disturbing the air. Liam frowned, but as no sign of activity was forthcoming he turned and rolled out of bed. He raked a hand through his hair, his brow furrowing as it seemed to take longer to do than normal, and shook his head. "Time to find some answers," he muttered.

Beware…Liam…

Liam jumped, glancing around the room. He was convinced he had heard someone speak – but no one was there. He gritted his teeth as he rubbed his forehead, but the whisper still reverberated through his mind. Perhaps this was all a dream. Yes, that fit – some crazy dream he'd had after falling and hitting his head. After all, there was no proof that any of it had happened – no hammer, no strange blue…glowing…light…

Liam stared at the door, underneath which the very light he'd just thought of gleamed. "Now that just isn't fair," he groaned as the door creaked inward. What stepped through it only served to further convince Liam of the insanity of his subconscious.

It was huge and unarguably male, clothed only in a tattered loincloth of some dark leather. It hunched forward as it squeezed through the door, and as it straightened Liam swallowed hard. The thing was huge, the tips of its horns scraping furrows in the ceiling as it loped forward. Its arms hung below its knees, long claws marring the tiled floor, and Liam saw that it was smiling grotesquely at him with teeth filed into points. Its body was covered in strange markings and swirling tattoos of an eerie blue that glowed sickly, and he was repulsed at the sight of it. How could he ever have thought it to be the same light that had emanated from his hammer?

Liam came to his senses as the creature uttered a deafening roar and charged forward. He raised his pistol and fired, the rounds exiting the chamber like lightning while thunder echoed through the room. The creature shrieked something in a deep, guttural language Liam could not understand as it fell, and for some reason its wounds seemed cauterized.

The meaning of the monster's cry became clear to Liam as two other creatures charged through the door, a third literally bursting through the wall. They were similar in appearance to the first, save that all three bore shields and weapons – two held spears and one grasped a wickedly curved knife. Rather than charging they circled forward, one carelessly stepping upon the body of his fallen comrade. Liam shot and missed, his hands shaking from the sudden cold that had entered the room with the giants. He could feel the sweat on his back freezing in the air, though the hand that held his gun was warm.

He backed up as he fired again, striking the arm of one of the spear-bearing giants. The creature let out a harsh bellow and Liam heard the wall behind him break. He swiveled around, firing blindly. A scream of pain informed him that he had struck another as he rolled on instinct, barely dodging the knife that swooped for his head as the giants closed in. He came up with his back to the corner and cursed softly as two more giants entered through the shattered wall, climbing over the corpse of what he took to be a female version of the monstrosities. Liam grimaced, knowing that the odds were not in his favor, and prepared to fight for his life as the giants charged, confident in their strength of numbers.

A high ululation suddenly sang through the bellows of the giants, and they turned as a figure blurred through their midst. It whirled and twisted, a fiery blade dancing through the creatures and the blue glow alike, and Liam lost some of the chill that had slowed him.

The figure came to a halt on the other side of the room as several of the giants dropped, felled by her blade. Liam saw a girl still in her late teens, her long blonde hair flowing to below her waist. She wore a suit of glinting mail belted around her waist, with loose black sweat pants and sneakers underneath. Her gloves were leather, as was the long duster she wore over her coat of mail. Her sword was held extended at her side, and it glowed with an orange flame that warmed the room.

The look on her lovely features was one of disdain as four more giants entered the room, all bearing cauterized wounds – and judging by the hateful looks they shot the girl, she was the responsible party. The four closed in on her as the remaining duo looked back to Liam, murder in their eyes as they charged. He fired rapidly, downing one as the girl cried out with a faintly British accent, "Use the hammer, you moron!"

"What – I don't have a hammer!" he yelled back, dropping to one knee as he continued firing. The giant blocked most of the shots with his shield, though he stumbled as one got through. Liam's chamber clicked empty and he cursed, not having enough time to reload.

The giant grinned as though it sensed victory and leapt at Liam. On instinct he repeated the move he had used on Kevin, whipping his pistol at the giant's knee.

About time! cheered the voice in his head, and Liam felt a distinct burst of glee that did not belong to him as time seemed to slow down. He felt his gun suddenly…change, the grip lengthening and gaining a cover of leather as the barrel grew thicker. The black morphed to a gleaming silver that glowed with the pure blue light of the cave, eliminating what little chill remained in the room. Though it felt as light as his .45, Liam somehow found himself holding the sledgehammer from the cavern.

Time returned to normal and the hammer connected with the giant's knee, sweeping him from his feet and sending him flying across the room, where he knocked into one of his brethren. The girl let out a breathless, high laugh, uttering her shrill cry again as she spun and decapitated one of the giants. Liam *felt* his hammer tug him to the side, and he dodged the blow his second opponent aimed for him with its bare fists. He turned his awkward dive into a roll and came out of it, throwing his hammer on a whim. It slammed into the center of his target with impossible force and went *through* it, sending a splatter of black gore onto the wall as the beast stumbled and fell still on the bed.

Liam dodged to the side as one of the girl's attackers split off and swung a backhanded blow at him. Not quite knowing why, the cop raised his hand and managed to catch his hammer as it flew back to him. Liam looked at it in surprise and felt a sharp shock run down his arm as his mysterious voice snapped *Idiot!*, the hammer shoving him to one side again. The giant's mallet slammed into the floor where he had stood a moment before, sending splinters of tile flying. Liam swiftly lashed out and downed the monster.

He rose warily and found the girl dispatching yet another – but behind her reared a third giant swinging for her, a fact to which she was seemingly oblivious. "Look out!" he yelled, gesturing with his hammer.

The girl dropped to the ground as the lights dimmed, several blowing out entirely. Liam's vision swam and the hair on his arms rose as *something* swept through him, a power that threw and deposited him firmly against the wall six feet back.

Several moments passed before Liam could see again, and when he could he found himself unable to move. Exhaustion greater than any he had ever known filled him, and he could only watch as the girl rose incredulously from the ground. She stared at the giant who stood behind her, examining the burnt hole that had hollowed out his middle and melted most of the ice in the room. The fluorescent lights above had burnt out, the only light in the room emanating from her sword and his hammer, though there was a faint glow of daylight that shone through one of the holes in the wall.

She turned and walked to Liam, shaking her head furiously. "You idiot," she muttered, her accent growing stronger with her anger. "What were you thinking, throwing lightning around like that? You could have killed me if I had not reacted in time!"

Liam stared at her for a moment before bursting into laughter. Somehow the events of the day seemed hilarious to him, and the puzzled look on her face only heightened his amusement. She raised one eyebrow and tapped her foot, waiting, and after a moment he sobered. "Sorry," he said when he had caught his breath. "I just find it amusing that you think I know how to use this thing."

Her eyes widened. "But you wield Mjolnir itself! Surely you must have received *some* training."

"Mjol- what is a Mjolnir?" he asked, butchering the pronunciation. Nothing about this day was making any sense, though given the soreness of his muscles and his utter exhaustion he was beginning to doubt that this was a dream.

She gazed at him with evident shock, opening and closing her mouth several times. Finally she spoke, her voice incredulous. "Mjolnir is the hammer of Thor, god of lightning – and for some reason, he has chosen to bestow it upon you."

Liam's eyebrows climbed. "Thor. Right. As in champion of Asgard, god of the Norse, most commonly seen in comics. Don't tell me superheroes are real."

It was the girl's turn to laugh. "Please! The original Thor, not the comic version. He is the basis for that character, the actual warrior." She shook her head and extended a hand to Liam, who grasped it, surprised at her strength as she hauled him to his feet. "You *have* heard the legends, have you not?

Liam shook his head. "Mythology never held much interest for me. What the hell were those things?" He still found it hard to believe that the monsters were not simply a nightmare.

"Frost giants of Jötunheimr," she replied, an underlying current of worry in her voice. "But I have never before seen them in this realm."

"Realm?"

"You would know it as a planet. I simply call it by the old term."

Liam groaned. "Look, this has been a crazy day, and nothing is making sense to me. Can you *please* just tell me what's going on?"

She frowned. "I am afraid there is little time for such things. I had assumed you would have a basic idea of where things stand, but it appears I was wrong. I cannot imagine what the Order was thinking…I will have to explain things as we ride, I fear."

"Ride? Ride what?" Something clicked in Liam's mind and he realized there was something familiar here. Thor, and Mjolnir – he had heard their names all too recently. After a moment he remembered. "Wait a minute! I dreamed about this!"

She turned and walked to the hole in the wall, nodding in satisfaction as she saw a faint trickle of sunlight ahead. "I would guess that your dream was a vision from the gods, chosen of Thor Odinson."

"What? I don't understand."

"You are the bearer of the hammer, gifted to you by the defender of Asgard." She heaved a sigh, and Liam thought that it conveyed far too much sorrow for one so young. "Everything will make sense in time, I promise, but for now I need you to trust me." She grimaced as she spoke, rubbing her shoulder blade as she uttered an almost inaudible curse.

Liam looked at her – this strange girl who had come out of nowhere and saved his life, who spoke nonsense but seemed to believe it, and who was his only hope of making sense out of any of the events of the day. After a moment he nodded. "Do I at least get to know your name?" he asked, struggling to act as though this was all normal.

She laughed, her gray eyes sparkling, and nodded her thanks. "I am called Solveig. And you?"

"Liam," he replied.

"Well, Liam, the first thing that I need you to do is to mask your hammer."

"I beg your pardon?"

She sighed. "Your hammer was a gun when I first entered the room; one of the first things you should have learned was how to shift your relic to a less conspicuous shape. A pistol, for example." Her own sword remained unmasked as she slid it into a sheathe at her side, the girl apparently confident in her ability to keep it hidden beneath her duster.

Less conspicuous. Right. Liam looked from her to the three foot long tool of destruction in his hand. *How in the world...*

Like this, said the voice, and the hammer suddenly shrank back into the shape of the gun. Liam jumped, almost losing his grip on the weapon, and once again he heard laughter within his head.

Solveig looked at him, her head cocked to one side. "You learn quickly," she murmured as Liam stared at her, his eyes wide.

The cop shook his head. "I don't think I have much choice in the matter."

She laughed. "Come, friend. We have far to travel, and little time in which to do so." She led him through the hole in the wall, walking through several more that made a path to the outside. There waited a horse, a beautiful creature of pure gray. He bore no saddle on his back and seemed content to graze upon the frost-dusted lawn outside of the hospital. As they approached he turned and greeted Solveig with a whinny, trotting towards her and nuzzling her.

Liam froze, staring at the horse as she whispered to it. "Um. Why does your horse have six legs?"

She looked at him, her eyes flashing with sudden fire. "His name is Gunnar, and he is a descendant of Sleipnir, the eight legged horse of Odin himself. There is no finer or faster creature in this realm. Do you have a problem with him?" For the first time, she sounded like a teenager.

Liam shook his head, forcing himself to tear his gaze from the animal. "No, no problem. Just...not what I was expecting."

Solveig sighed. "I apologize. I understand that this must have been a trying day for you, but Gunnar often receives such reactions, and I am... somewhat defensive of him. Pray forgive me."

Gunnar whickered and nibbled on Solveig's hair. Liam laughed and reached out to awkwardly pat the horse's neck. "There's nothing to forgive – I'm sorry I gawked. I've never been much of a horse person."

She looked at him with a wicked smile. "Then the next few hours will not be overly pleasant for you, I am afraid. Mount up."

Liam blinked. "Wait, *this* is our ride?"

Her smile grew. "Yes. He is faster than any manmade car or train, and using him will not endanger the lives of civilians – a fact that I am certain you will appreciate, being a protector of the innocent."

Liam swallowed heavily and nodded, thinking that her words made sense. No chance of endangering civilians would be good…but still, a horse?

It took him several tries to mount up, even with Solveig's assistance. She mounted easily after him, swinging up as though her mail suit did not hinder her at all. She wrapped one arm around Liam's waist to brace him and clucked at Gunnar, her disdain for reins evident by the lack of them as she nudged the horse with her knees. At once they were off, and Liam bit back a yelp as the wind whipped his hair into his face.

He frowned for a moment, confused by its length, and realized that his beard too had lengthened. "Can you tell me what the deal is with my hair?" he yelled back to Solveig.

She chuckled. "A simple question, but I fear you jump straight into the heart of the issue. Every time you draw upon Thor's powers you become closer to him, in both looks and in knowledge. Those who use the relics of the gods for extended periods of time tend to become more and more similar to their god or goddess."

"And what if I don't want to be like this 'god'?"

Ha! Who wouldn't?

Solveig shrugged. "I understand your dilemma, but it is not a bad thing. You will not become Thor himself – you will merely gain some of his powers and knowledge, in return sacrificing some of your appearance. The negative aspects are purely cosmetic, I assure you."

Liam frowned over that for a moment before deciding to drop the issue in lieu of more important things. "I'm a Christian – understand that I have some difficulty believing in these 'gods' of yours."

He felt Solveig shake her head behind him. "God with a capital G is different than that of which I speak. These beings I refer to as gods are not akin to your God; they simply bear the name because no other could be found to describe them in the time that they walked the earth. You would understand them better as aliens, I think, but even that is not entirely accurate. They are like you, but not of this world, and infinitely more advanced than you are – perhaps not scientifically, but in knowledge and power, and they possess extended lifespans."

Liam groaned, trying to wrap his mind around the strange concept. "Okay. So we're dealing with aliens. I think I can manage that. But back to my beard for a moment – can I shave it off?"

Shave it?!? Shave it?!?! What sort of man are you, to shave your beard!

Solveig laughed. "You could," she replied, "but it would only grow back the next time you used your hammer."

And for the better!

The cop snorted. "What about this voice in my head? What's that?"

He felt her stiffen behind him. "A voice? What does it say?"

"Mostly derisive comments, though it had a few useful ones during the battle. At the moment," Liam shook his head, trying to quiet the protests, "It's insisting that it's very useful and that I'm a daft idiot."

Solveig let out a soft whistle. "It is said that those who have possessed their relics for the longest can hear the voices of their gods, most often in their dreams. Never before have I heard of one whose relic was so recently claimed hearing their god; but then again, so powerful a relic has never before been recorded in the hands of a mortal." She paused for a moment, her next words uncertain. "I believe that you are hearing Thor."

"So I'm hearing voices. But I'm not crazy."

"Not at all. I would advise listening to him most carefully – if he speaks to you now, with such events afoot, he may offer aid."

Liam nodded, and then realized that he had missed something. "Hold on a moment – did you say there were others? And what are these 'relics'?"

"Well, yes! You did not think you were the first, did you?" She took his silence as answer enough and shook her head, continuing, "I cannot offer you the full history, only the most basic idea of events that have transpired. Long ago the gods – or, if you prefer, the Æsir – walked the earth, aiding mankind with their dilemmas. They have since vanished back to Asgard, their home, but pieces of their passing have been left behind. These are what we call relics. They have been found by humans throughout the years, and have inevitably left their mark on history."

"Some of these relics are passed down as family heirlooms, along with the tales of their former wielders, the Æsir. Others are found and then lost in passing, only to be rediscovered years later. There is a group that has dedicated their lives to the finding and safekeeping of these relics, swearing to only use them for good and to not meddle in the affairs of mortals. The Order created 'Seekers', those whose relics gave them the powers to travel great distances swiftly, or to glimpse images of the future – these Seekers seek out new relic bearers to invite them to join the Order." She paused for a moment. "In truth, I am surprised they did not find you – such a powerful relic should have been seen coming."

Liam could sense that this bothered her, but she shrugged it off and continued. "There have, of course, been a few who have received invitations to the Order but chose to decline them, using their relics with their own judgment – it was these people who first inspired your legends of 'superheroes'. Some, however, have chosen to use their relics for evil. The other relic bearers then band together to stop them."

The cop's head swam with the information. "And…are you a part of this organization?"

"I am not." Solveig's voice was sharp, and Liam sensed he'd touched upon a delicate subject. "I do not bear a relic, and they will not accept those without one."

"But, your sword – it was on fire. Is that normal?"

Her voice softened into a more wistful tone. "A family heirloom, but never a tool of the gods. It is called Gram."

Liam nodded, not fully understanding but also not wanting to push the issue further. "Then if you're not a Seeker, how did you know where to find me?"

"There lies a mystery for both of us, I fear. I received a letter two days ago, unmarked save for the crest of a raven. It instructed me to head to the Caves of the Colossus this morning. I set off at once and arrived just in time to see you struck by lightning. You collapsed, and I carried you to the hospital. I'm afraid I did not factor in the time difference between our zones." She sounded ashamed, and Liam bit back a laugh.

"Then you were the angel Kevin saw! But – you said that relics as powerful as mine are rarely found. Why was it just lying around in Colossal Cave?"

"That I cannot answer either. Mjolnir is Thor's hammer, a weapon he will sorely need at some point in the future – I cannot imagine him ever willingly parting with it, but nor can I see it being taken from him. I called you his chosen because that is the only thing I can think of – that he chose you to bear his weapon for some reason we cannot see. The only other time I can recall where something this powerful was gifted to humans was when some Greek fellow named Herakles discovered Thor's belt of strength. Normally relics are merely fragments of their original self. Perhaps you should ask Thor."

Liam exhaled slowly. *Oookay*, he thought. *How does one talk to an alien?*

Just like that.

He jumped. *You can hear me?*

*Obviously. Know this, my friend – the time is not yet come for all to be revealed. Wait until the Lifkyr's task has been completed; then all shall make sense. As for now, I am busy. Do **try** to stay out of trouble, won't you?*

Liam groaned at the condescending tone. "He…um. He says that 'the time has not yet come' for us to know, and that something called a Lifkyr has to finish its task? Oh, and he told us to stay out of trouble."

Solveig stiffened. "You can communicate that eloquently with him? For the message to come through so clearly…things here are very strange. There is much going on that is hidden from us, but he is correct in one thing – our task is not yet completed."

"What do you mean? And where are we going?"

"The same note that told me to meet you also said that by tomorrow morning at four of the clock we must be in New York City – and it specified an address to be at."

Liam blinked. New York City was over 2,000 miles away, and they had less than twelve hours to get there. "So we're going by horse?"

She laughed. "Look down, my friend. Do you still doubt that we can make it?"

His eyes widened as he glanced downward and found the earth far below them, the landscape flashing by as Gunnar seemed to run upon thin air.

Moonday

I'm standing on the edge of a ledge, backing away from the shadows that advance before me. The last vestiges of light are focused on where I stand now, and as the terror engulfs me, they fade. I am bathed in darkness and I fall into it, screaming, clutching for something, anything to grab on to...

Elena awoke to the vibrations of her phone upon her stomach. A car alarm sounded in the distance as she stood, dressing quietly in the near darkness of her room. Down the hall she could hear her father's quiet snores, so much softer now than they had been. Silently she grabbed her bag, prepared hours ago, and crept out of the window.

It was three stories to the ground, and Elena was glad to have the fire escape to aid her in her descent. No one was in sight as she reached the bottom, but she tucked her long black hair into a tail nonetheless and pulled up the hood of her black jacket. She began to walk, keeping her head down and trying to blend into the background as much as possible. New York City was not a place she much cared to walk at night, particularly alone, but she had little choice in the matter.

Several blocks later she reached her destination. The house was large, the marble pillars out in the front marking it as belonging to someone very rich and with little interest in blending into the neighborhood. She shook her head as she walked past it to the opposite street corner, where there stood a tall library that would have looked grand were it beside anything but the mansion.

Elena rounded the corner and came to the fire ladder, climbing swiftly for several minutes until she reached the top of the building. She kept to the shadows as much as possible, her soft ballet slippers – also black - offering little protection to her feet from the deep chill of the snow that blanketed the roof – but they made no sound. Elena nodded in satisfaction as she reached the edge, looking out at the street below her. There was no traffic, and she took a moment to catch her breath before reaching into her bag.

Carefully she pulled out the homemade grappling hook, pieced together out of several thick metal coat hangers and a rope left over from her days of rock climbing. She secured one end tightly around the balcony of the roof and began to spin the rope, praying she'd followed the directions her internet search had given her well enough. Elena tossed the hook out and let the rope play through her fingers, watching breathlessly as it landed with a soft clatter on the top of the mansion's roof.

"Excellent," she murmured, tugging gently on the rope until it caught upon the elegant parapet that surrounded the roof. She tugged harder, finally confident that it was well and truly stuck. Taking a deep breath, she made sure the rope was taught before wrapping her hands around the zipline attached at her end. She took another three or four deep breaths – *just to be on the safe side* – before she realized she was delaying the moment.

Here we go! she thought, and pushed off the roof. She flew across the street, fighting the urge to scream as she extended her feet to take the impact of the mansion wall that rushed up to meet her. The realization that she had bitten her tongue came with the blood that pooled in her mouth. Elena hung there panting breathlessly until her arms began to burn from the strain, only then forcing herself to move. Carefully she lowered herself onto the ledge, leaving her zipline hanging from the rope as an escape route. She began to creep towards the nearest window, which repeated observation from the library had told her led directly to the study.

Elena used her hands to aid her as she snuck along, confident that her black gloves would keep her from leaving fingerprints. She reached the window and stayed to one side of it in case someone should pass by, carefully lowering one hand into her bag and pulling out a paperclip. She partially unfolded the first bend, inserting it into the crack in the pane as her books had told her to. Gently she pushed upwards until she felt resistance from the bolt, at which point she shoved it upwards and finagled with it until she heard a soft click as the lock unlatched.

The window opened outwards, so she twisted the paperclip until the partial bend was to the side, hoping that the owner kept his hinges well oiled. Elena pulled on the clip and smiled as the pane opened, taking one last quick peek inside before she shimmied in. It was dark within, and she took a moment for her vision to adjust before closing the window behind her.

She knew herself to now be in the private study of the owner, where there stood a great many bookcases full of antiques that he never touched. They were there purely for show, a fact which horrified Elena. Several of the books would sell for thousands of dollars to collectors who would actually treasure them for what they were, and she would see to it that the money went to a good cause.

Elena clicked on the red light that hung from her belt, covered with a thin black cloth that dimmed the lighting even more. Though still bright enough by which to see basic shapes and to read by at close distance, it was less likely to be seen than a brighter light – or so her research had informed her. Elena closed the distance to the bookshelves and began to peruse them , struggling against the temptation to open a few of the rarer ones and sneak a peek for herself. This was not an academic trip, after all.

Seeing one of the books which she sought was on the top shelf, Elena hissed in dismay. She was short, far too tiny to hope to reach it without aid. She immediately dismissed the heavy chair that sat behind the oak desk as too difficult to move, and realized that she would have to search for a stepladder elsewhere. The room a nearby doorway led to, full of an extensive collection of antiques there simply to impress any who should happen to pass through, seemed the best place to start. Elena headed through the doorway, feeling for some reason that this was *definitely* the right way to go.

Liam and Solveig arrived at the library rooftop only to find that someone else had been there before them. It was not quite four, and Liam was sore in spots he didn't know he could be thanks to the long ride, but he had to admit – Gunnar had gotten them there. Solveig was still smug from her victory, but she too looked surprised when they saw the grappling hook.

Uttering a soft curse, the cop traced it to the building on the opposite corner. It was a huge house, made of white marble that looked expensive – and, in this neighborhood, tasteless. "This is way out of my district – I don't have authority here," he murmured to Solveig, shivering. He'd thought that Tucson was cold, but it had *nothing* on New York.

She shrugged in response, uninterested as she perched in the snow. "It does not concern us. Our task is to wait here until four."

Liam's eyes widened in surprise. "There's a crime taking place in that building – look! I can see the red light! We can't just stand by and let this happen."

"What would you have us do? As you said, you have no authority in this place, and no phone with which to call the police. Besides, do you not think they would wonder why we were here?"

Liam grimaced. "Well, I can't just sit here. You stay here and wait for whoever's supposed to show up; I'm going in."

Solveig stood in amazement as he swung over the edge of the balcony, wrapping both hands around the rope and swinging out over the street. "And just what are you going to do?" she whispered fiercely.

"My job!" he called back, moving hand over hand.

With a groan she watched him reach the edge and slink along the wall to the window that was partially open. The would-be thief chose that moment to exit the room, and Liam softly tugged open the window. He waved at Solveig before entering and vanished into the darkness after the thief.

Muttering to herself, Solveig looked around, then at her watch. She still had a few minutes before four – she supposed it would be enough time to try and keep him out of trouble.

Elena walked through the near darkness, the street lights outside blocked by tinted windows so that all she could make out were darkened shapes. There was a creak from behind her and she whirled, freezing, but saw nothing. After a moment she turned back and began to walk once more, her red light guiding her.

No ladder or stool was immediately visible, but Elena chose to remain positive and walked towards the darkest corner. Something about it seemed to say, *Over here. Try me.* She crept across the wooden floor and peered into the shadows, finding-

Still nothing! Elena groaned. It seemed she would be forced to leave behind the treasured manuscript and take some of those that rested nearer her height. Shaking her head, she started to turn – and paused as her flashlight caught on something. It was shoved underneath a short table display, almost out of sight, and she couldn't help but wonder why. A closer inspection proved that the item was a pair of sandals, small and remarkably tasteful for this collection.

She glanced around and decided that she had time for a quick peek. Elena knelt and peered under the table, shining her light directly on the shoes. They were an old type of sandal, with laces that went up almost to the knee. Made of a leather so dark it was almost black, intricate stitching decorated every inch. The shadows were dark under the table, and her light barely illuminated the stitches.

Elena grimaced, inexplicably desperate to see what the patterns were despite her circumstances. These shoes had a story to them, of that she was certain, and if she could but see them a little better she felt certain she would learn it. Perhaps the light by the window would be better suited? She dimly heard the bells of the church several blocks away chime four as she stretched out her hand, reaching for the shoes. Elena could almost swear she heard a woman whisper, "No! Do *not* touch-," but it was too late.

As her hand fell upon the leather Elena heard a soft chuckle, and then everything went black.

I watch as the idiots race up the hill, thinking that they can catch me – me! The fools. Would I have picked so obvious of a hiding spot if I did not have a means of escape?

I wait until the last possible moment, hoping to make them think that they actually stand half a chance; after all, that's half the fun. Finally I whirl dramatically, dashing out the door that leads to the Glittering Force and its pond. I race along the riverbed, jumping out over the waterfall, and as I do I feel my skin morph, shifting into shining scales. I immerse myself in the cool blue water and lurk at the bottom of the pond, laughing.

They are detained at the house for several minutes, and I can only imagine their confusion. At last I see them at the top of the waterfall, and they begin to descend the slippery rocks as carefully as they can. Several times they almost fall, and I can only dream of how glorious a happenstance that would be – but alas, it appears one god is all I am allowed to slay…at least for now.

Finally they reach the bottom, and I see them look to the pond. Their mouths move, but beneath the water sound is distorted, and I cannot make out what they are saying. No matter; it is of little consequence to me.

Kvasir passes something to Thor, and I begin to wonder if he knows that I watch them. Of the two of them, his presence worries me the most, for next to me he is the cleverest of the gods. But then again, Thor is here, and he could not bear to have someone else in charge. I rest secure in the knowledge of my safety.

They circle around to opposite ends of the pond, and I see something glimmering above me, near the surface. Curious, I dart towards it, using my tail to propel me. There is no danger to me – I know that they cannot possibly hope to harm me.

The pattern confuses me and I twist my head, cursing the difference between these fishy eyes and my normal ones. Clear squares of sunlight, bordered by a pattern of shadow…realization dawns and I twist to return to the bottom, but it is too late! Kvasir sweeps the net – one of my own making, damn their arrogance! – underneath me, and I realize I am caught.

Desperately I swim towards Thor, whom I deem to be the lesser of two evils. Kvasir has proven to be too cunning for me this day. I see the faintest opening left, a small glimmer of escape still shining, and I leap from the waters as I desperately try to transform-

But Thor has caught me, dropping the net to do so. His hands tighten around me, but he does not seek to crush me. I sense his true purpose as he lifts me high above the water, depriving me of its cool depths as my gills begin to burn. He means to suffocate me!

I writhe and twist, desperately trying to escape, but his grip is too strong. My vision begins to fade to black, and I fear that this may be the end of me. To be defeated by such a hot-headed fool – surely this cannot be!

My salvation comes from an unlikely place. Kvasir appears in my shrinking tunnel of vision, gripping Thor's shoulder. "Enough!" he cries. "You know your father's command!"

Odin! My blood brother! Of course, he cannot bear to see me killed. I relax slightly, but pray that Thor comes to see reason before it is too late. Slowly, ever so slowly, his grip loosens. I return to my normal shape before he can change his mind, relishing the air I can now suck in.

Kvasir squeezes Thor's shoulder, and the big, burly god of thunder grimaces. "You're right," he finally mutters, still gripping my arm in a painful vice. "Just as my father is right. Death is too good for this one."

The meaning behind his words reaches me, and I pause in my exultation. Perhaps my salvation is not so glorious as I had supposed…

But little do the fools know that this is not the extent of my plans.

The blinking red light that appeared next to Liam was instantly recognizable as a silent alarm, but just now he was more worried about the would-be thief. She had been rummaging around in some darkened corner, but had suddenly collapsed into the darkness. "What happened?" he hissed at Solveig, his heart still racing from her sudden appearance behind him.

She cursed, the vulgarity sounding strange on her normally eloquent tongue. "We have found who we were sent for."

Liam blinked. "What? The thief?"

Solveig grimaced. "Another newly in possession of a relic, it would seem."

He looked back to where the woman lay sprawled on the ground. Her appearance was about what he'd expect from a crook – a black jacket with the hood pulled up to hide her face, gloves and loose pants that were easy to move in, a small bag to carry tools of the trade and any items picked up. The only thing out of place were her shoes, some sort of flat sandal that laced up to her knees. They didn't seem to fit with her outfit, especially in weather like this.

"The shoes?" he asked tentatively, wondering if they might qualify as a relic.

Solveig nodded. "I was trying to prevent her from touching them, but it appears I was a moment too late. We must get her out of here."

"Can't we just leave her for the cops? She *was* trying to steal them."

The blonde shook her head. "The note specified that I must bring two to our next destination."

Liam's confusion grew. "Wait – this isn't it? I thought this was where we were supposed to be!"

"This was but the first of our stops. I am now instructed to take the two of you to a hotel on the outskirts of the city. This would prove difficult to do if she was imprisoned, and since I can hear the sirens in the distance, I suggest we move quickly."

Liam cocked his head and listened for a moment, catching a hint of the familiar noise. He cursed but picked up the woman's limp body, heaving it over one shoulder. The silent alarm flashed bright in the darkness and he turned to Solveig, all thoughts of stealth now forgotten.

"How do we get out?" he asked.

She shrugged. "Perhaps the way we came in."

Liam grimaced but turned to the main study, letting Solveig lead the way through the darkness.

They came to a halt next to the window through which they had entered and the woman opened it carefully, checking outside for the patrol cars Liam was sure would soon arrive. For now there was no sign of them, and he carefully steadied the limp girl on his shoulder as Solveig helped them through the window.

Going along the ledge was tricky, but somehow they made it to the rope. The sirens were louder now, closing the distance to the mansion swiftly. Liam shot a nervous glance at Solveig.

"I think I can make it down with her," he called above the howling wind, "but I'm going to need your help, and you're going to have to climb down!"

She shrugged. "I have my own means of escape already planned, thank you. But I shall assist you as I can."

Liam exhaled and nodded, wishing that she would talk like a normal person. "I'm going to grab the rope – I need you to cut it from where it's attached to the roof."

She glanced up as realization dawned. "And then you shall swing to the ground; I see. Are you sure you can bear the woman?"

Liam nodded his assent and she drew her sword, the flames paler seemingly in deference to their need for stealth. Liam shifted his hold on the girl and grabbed the rope tightly, wrapping it once around his fist. Solveig waited until he nodded and then cut the rope.

Liam bit back a yelp as he jumped off of the edge, clinging tightly to both the rope and the girl. They glided across empty space for a few moments before his feet hit the ground near the center of the road, the woman still completely limp on his shoulder. Liam skidded across the snow for a few feet before stopping near the wall of the library they'd landed at earlier. He glanced behind him, worried as to how Solveig would make her descent – and felt his jaw drop at what he saw.

Solveig seemed to walk on thin air, descending as though on invisible steps. A faint purple glow lit her back, and for a moment Liam thought he could make out the shape of wings. Then she landed beside him, and the light disappeared. She chuckled at the look of shock on his face. "As I said, I have no need of help."

Liam nodded, averting his eyes to where Gunnar raced to meet them so he didn't stare at her. As far as the events of the day were concerned, this was hardly the strangest thing he had seen, but it was still somewhat shocking. "So what now?" he asked.

"Now we go to the motel," she replied.

Liam bit back a laugh, glancing about nervously as the sirens drew closer. "Um. I hate to break it to you, but there are an awful lot of motels around here."

Solveig raised an eyebrow. "Please. I have the address."

"Gotcha." Liam sighed, looking at Gunnar and wondering if the horse would be able to carry three. "And where do we go from there?"

"We do not. We stay the night, and there our instructions end. Our room should be paid for." Solveig glanced around. "But I think we had better leave quickly." At Liam's nod, she mounted her horse gracefully, reaching down and helping him to haul the woman up behind her. Liam was left to mount on his own, which he did with considerably less panache. Gunnar whickered at the weight of the trio, but still stood steady.

They left at a gallop just as the first flashing lights rounded the corner.

Though New York had seen some strange things in its days, Liam was fairly certain that a six-legged horse galloping through traffic while bearing a cop and two women, one of them in chain mail and the other unconscious, was among the oddest. He was grateful for Gunnar's speed, which had them across town in several minutes and left them a blur that he hoped made identifying them difficult.

Solveig dismounted first, instructing Gunnar and Liam to wait while she headed in to get their keys. The motel looked just like any other of its kind, though the snow blanketing the roof was a first for Liam, who was used to dry heat. He had just managed to get the woman off of the horse when Solveig returned, room key held triumphantly in her hand.

"Wait, it actually was reserved?" he asked her, surprised.

She blinked. "Yes, as I told you it was."

"Right. What name was it under?"

"High," she replied.

"High? Just High?" Liam groaned. He had hoped for a clue as to who had led them on this ridiculous odyssey. "Did they leave a message?"

Solveig shook her head, grabbing the woman from him and shouldering her with no apparent effort. "Come. We are in room seventeen."

She turned and began to walk towards it, but Liam grabbed her arm. When she shot him an annoyed look he pointed to the horse. "What about Gunnar?"

She raised her eyebrows. "What about him?"

Liam glanced towards where the horse stood, centered in one of the slots of the parking lot, and fought a laugh. "Well, he kinda stands out, and if the cops caught a glimpse of him before we left…"

"Ah, a good point," Solveig replied, walking towards Gunnar. She stroked his muzzle and whispered to him for a moment before backing away. The horse reared and whinnied at them before galloping out into traffic, running a red light and nearly causing an accident before he disappeared from their view. Solveig nodded in satisfaction. "He will come when we call."

Liam thought silence was the best answer and instead merely nodded, hiding his grin as he followed her to the room. Perhaps inside they would find their next clue.

The room was spartan but sufficient, with a small bathroom and shower off to one side and two beds. There was only one thing out of place, a card that Liam was sure the cleaning staff had not left. Strange runes stood out from the heavy paper.

"What in the world is that?" he asked as Solveig tossed the woman onto one of the beds. She turned quizzically and picked up the card, giving the runes a quick glance. " 'Sleep well,'" she murmured. "It would appear we have our next task."

Liam groaned. "Could they be any more cryptic?" he muttered.

"Yes." The answer surprised him and he looked at Solveig, who bore a dry smile.

"Was that a joke?" he asked incredulously. He hadn't thought her capable of joking.

"Yes," she replied, her smile growing. "But also a truth."

Liam shook his head, chuckling, and walked towards the bathroom. "Sleep, huh," he called back. "Do you know, I'm actually inclined to go along with this one – but first, I find a razor."

When he emerged freshly shaven he found Solveig asleep on a chair in the corner of the room, her chain mail folded neatly beside her. She was dressed in simple sweats and a tank top, and she looked smaller this way, more fragile. It struck Liam again how young she was.

Shaking his head he gently picked her up, walking her to the second bed and carefully laying her on it before claiming her chair. He pulled his gun from its holster and examined it, frowning with concentration until it shifted once more into his hammer. He stared at it for a few minutes before setting it aside, finally caving in to his exhaustion.

I watch in satisfaction as Loki is dragged kicking and screaming to the rocks I have positioned. It was hard, so hard, to let him live after what he has done, but my father is right. Death, even with all of the tortures that await him in Hel, would be too kind for him. Instead we have devised our own punishment.

His sons, of course, were furious at his capture and foolishly sought to free him. Using their own entrails to bind him to his tomb seems fitting after his betrayal. I watch as Loki is bound, his once handsome face now wild, his true side showing in this moment when all is lost, and I take pleasure in seeing the serpent unmasked.

Eyes pleading, he looks to my father. Out of all of us, this betrayal must hurt Odin the most, for he had sworn a blood-bond to Loki. "Brother, please!" the fiend cries out, but my father's eyes are hard. Many transgressions has he forgiven the mischief maker in the past, but with Baldr's murder, Loki has crossed a line from which he may not return. I look on in satisfaction as Odin turns away, and I see the realization strike Loki more truly than any lightning I can throw – he is alone, and none of us will mourn his loss.

Skaði steps forward with her offering for this prison, the final touch that is needed – a snake from her homeland that wields a corrosive poison. Her face is grim as she wraps the serpent above Loki, winding it tightly around the roots that hang overhead. She binds it there, and in its agony it begins to drip its venom.

Loki screams and writhes as the poison strikes his face, twisting until the very ground shakes – and I am shocked to hear a sob from our midst. I watch in disbelief as Sigyn dashes forward, falling to her knees before the stones. Tears stream down her face as she calls out to my father. "All-Father! Odin, please, wait!"

He turns to her, his face unsurprised, if marked with hints of disappointment. "I know what you would ask of me, Sigyn. But consider what he has done-"

Her eyes flash, and her voice is strong and proud. "He is still my husband. Nothing he can ever do will change that."

Loki's screams are all that is heard as my father considers. Finally he bows his head with a sigh. He moves his hands in a sure motion and a bowl appears before Sigyn. "I wish you well," he murmurs as she scrambles for it, grasping the bowl and running to hold it over Loki's face. It takes him a moment to realize that the poison no longer falls upon him. When he does, he stares up at Sigyn as she catches the drops, a look of utter surprise on his face.

Shaking my head, I follow the others out of the cave. Sif grasps my hand and I force a smile at her, knowing that we share the same wish – that Sigyn had chosen one more worthy of her loyalty.

We fall behind the others. "How is he?" my wife asks.

I take a moment to consider, the second presence in the back of my mind still strange to me. "Sleeping," I reply after a moment. "I think he can hear us."

She smiles up at me. "Hello, Liam."

"Liam. Liam!"

Liam awoke to a sharp voice and a hand shaking his shoulder. Eyes wide, he stared at Solveig, who looked at him with concern. "Are you alright?" she asked.

"I – yeah. Why, what's wrong?"

"You were shaking," she replied, sitting on the edge of the bed. Liam glanced around, taking a moment to remember where they were while he stretched, his back stiff from sitting all night. "Was it a nightmare?" Her voice was sympathetic.

"Yes…and no. I – I think I can see what Thor sees when I'm asleep."

She nodded. "If you can hear him so clearly in waking, it would not surprise me. Some relic bearers have reported seeing snippets of what they thought were the god's lives when dreaming. What did you see?"

"There was a man – Loki, I think his name was." Her face hardened, but she nodded for him to continue. "He'd done something, and they were punishing him; he was chained, and they were dropping acid on him or something. Thor seemed pretty happy about it."

Solveig grimaced. "Was there a snake over his head?"

Liam nodded. "Yeah, it was dripping poison, that's it! But how did you know?"

"Loki's betrayal and punishment have been foretold for years. If it has finally come…I may know why we have been contacted. What else did you see?"

Liam shrugged. "Not much. There was a woman, I think she was his wife, who begged to be allowed to help Loki. This big dude with white hair and one eye, Thor's dad, granted her permission. Oh, and Thor's wife said hi to me."

Her eyebrows climbed. "Really. The 'big dude', as you call him, is Odin, the king of all the gods. Did he give Sigyn a basin?"

"Yes. So, all of this has been foretold? How?"

Solveig sighed heavily. "Odin can see the future. The legends say that he warned mankind years ago of what would come to pass in Asgard – the realm of the gods," she added hastily as Liam opened his mouth. "The tales have been passed down for generations, and are considered mere fairytales now."

Liam thought for a moment. "Before, when I was at the hospital, I saw something else. I think it was an old funeral. There was a body and a pyre on a boat, and Thor was blessing it. Is that in the myths too?"

Solveig gaped at him. "The funeral of Baldr?" she asked in shock. "That was the vision the gods sent you?"

"Yeah! Isn't he Thor's brother? And…hold on a minute, I think Thor said something about Loki killing him!"

She stood, beginning to pace. "If Baldr is truly slain then events are worse than I had thought. It means that…that-"

"That the Ragnarök is begun," said a soft voice from behind her. Both jumped, having forgotten their companion. She sat up in bed, her eyes sleepy and her hair disheveled. "It's funny you should be talking about Norse mythology – I just dreamt of it. Where am I, please?"

"You dreamt of it?" Solveig asked, sitting on the woman's bed. Liam leaned forward. "What did you see?"

The woman shrugged. "It was strange, it was like I was Loki. It was him after Baldr's murder, trying to escape from the gods but being captured. Not my favorite myth, but hey – my subconscious obviously likes it."

Liam watched as Solveig's eyes dropped to the woman's shoes. "From Loki's point of view…" she murmured, staring.

"Sorry, again – where am I?" the girl repeated.

"It's…kind of complicated," Liam began when Solveig seemed unlikely to answer. The girl looked at him politely.

Just then, there came a loud knock on the door. Solveig stood immediately, hand falling to her sword. Liam glanced at the clock. "Just after nine," he read. "Too early for checkout."

Solveig nodded, her hair falling in a curtain as she did so. She brushed it back with a frustrated sigh as she walked to the door, the other woman looking at her with interest.

"Is that a real sword?" she asked, staring, but Solveig hushed her.

Liam followed her lead and grabbed his hammer from the table, praying he wouldn't do something stupid with it. Solveig nodded to him as he moved forward to support her, and she waited until he was in place to fling open the door.

Behind it stood a huge man with ebony skin and arms thicker than Liam's neck. He towered over the duo, his shadow falling through the door, but his voice was polite and surprisingly soft when he spoke. "Excuse me, miss, but are you Solveig?" he rumbled.

"Who is asking?" she challenged as his eyes dropped to her sword, and then to Liam around the door, his hammer clearly visible. The man chuckled softly.

"I'm guessing I'm in the right place, then. I'm Kieth, and I was told to meet you here." He reached into his pocket, and Liam grabbed Solveig's shoulder as she tensed. Something told him the man wasn't pulling a weapon.

Instead he produced a thick white piece of parchment, folded neatly with an emblem of a raven clearly visible on the top. The same runes from the card in the motel room were partially visible, and Liam jumped as a voice asked, "Ooh, are those Elder Futhark?" He hadn't noticed the woman rise to join them.

Solveig relaxed visibly at the sight of the card. "Perhaps it would be best if we continued this conversation inside," she murmured, stepping aside.

The man nodded his thanks. "That might be wise," he replied as he ducked through the door.

The room was crowded with four people in it, especially since both Kieth and the strange woman chose to stand. She looked on curiously as the man handed Solveig his letter, and she pored over it for a moment.

Liam glanced at the two strangers only to find the woman watching him. "Forgive me, but you're a cop. Why am I here and not in jail?" Her tone was matter of fact, and Liam was surprised at her composure when she spoke of prison.

Solveig answered before he could. "Because we have need of you." She carefully folded the letter and handed it back to Kieth, who pocketed it with a nod of thanks.

"Right. Can I call a lawyer?"

"This is outside the laws of mortals, I'm afraid." Kieth looked at her with some sympathy. "You might want to sit down for this."

She did so with a sigh, and Liam saw her eyebrows rise in surprise. "Who changed my shoes? Wait a minute, aren't these the ones from that collection?"

Liam bit back a laugh, now seeing his own position from the outside. He sat back as Solveig began to explain. "You seem to have some knowledge of the gods. Tell me, are you familiar with the term 'relic'?"

The girl shrugged. "You mean mortals who have found things that used to belong to the gods? Sure, there's a lot of myths about that. What does it have to do with anything?"

Solveig nodded to Liam, who raised his hammer. The girl glanced at it, and he saw her eyes widen as Kieth let out a soft whistle.

"Is that…Mjolnir?" he asked, his voice low.

The girl shook her head. "Impossible," she breathed, standing. "May I?"

Liam rose and extended the handle to her. As she reached for it Solveig warned, "It may be heavy."

Liam let go of the hammer and it dropped to the floor, the woman gasping as it pulled her arms with it. Kieth lunged forward but was too slow to catch it. "Sorry!" the girl gasped. "How do you carry that thing?"

Liam frowned. "I didn't think it was that heavy."

Solveig hid a smile with her hand. "Thor traditionally had to wear a belt and gauntlets that increased his strength in order to wield Mjolnir. I am not sure how you can carry it without them."

Well, I'm not giving you my entire wardrobe. It seemed more efficient to lend you a bit of my strength.

Liam laughed, stopping as the others stared at him. "Sorry, he, um…he says he's not giving me all of his clothes."

Kieth glanced at Solveig. "They can communicate?"

She nodded. "And he has begun to dream."

The woman glanced up from where she knelt by the hammer, examining it. "Okay, back up for a minute. Can someone please explain what's going on?"

Kieth sat down as Liam knelt to pick up his hammer. "We're still trying to figure that out. It seems none of us hold all the answers."

"Then maybe you should start at the beginning," the girl retorted, arching one eyebrow.

Solveig chuckled. "She is taking this more calmly than you did," she murmured to Liam, who snorted. "Very well," she added in a louder voice. "It began for me three days ago when I received a letter telling me to meet a man in the Caves of the Colossus-"

"Colossal Cave," Liam interjected. "In Arizona." The woman looked at him in surprise.

Solveig shot a glower at him as Kieth bit back a laugh. "That is what I said. I left from London and arrived a few minutes late due to different time zones. I found Liam unconscious and bearing the hammer, at which point I carried him to the hospital. There I left him in an unoccupied room and went to find a doctor. Several hallways down I was attacked by Jötun, and I returned to aid Liam."

Kieth sat up. "Jötun in Midgard? Are you sure?"

She blinked at him. "They are hard to mistake."

"Jötun are apparently frost giants," Liam said to the woman, who was following the duo's conversation.

She smiled at him. "Actually, Jötun is a generic name for all giants. There are different sub-species within, such as frost, fire, and earth."

Liam stared at her. "How do you know all of this?"

She shrugged. "I read."

Kieth took over. "I also received a letter, but not until yesterday evening. It told me to come here and meet a woman named Solveig, who would have two relic bearers with her."

"This has been bothering me," Liam interjected. "The two of you randomly received these anonymous letters with cryptic instructions and followed them without knowing why - or who they were from?"

"Oh, no," Kieth replied, his voice grave. "We knew who they were from."

"But-" Liam turned to Solveig. "You said the letter was unmarked."

"Save for the crest of a raven," she replied. The other woman's eyes widened in sudden understanding.

Liam frowned. "The raven? What does that have to do with anything?"

Kieth chuckled. "You don't know much about the Norse, do you?" he asked.

Solveig shook her head. "Which shall make this more difficult, I fear," she sighed.

It was the strange woman who took pity on him. "The raven is the sign of Odin – king of the gods."

"Who is also known in Midgard as High," Solveig added.

Liam blinked as his mind connected the dots. "The king of the gods rented us a room…at a motel."

Kieth and the woman laughed, though she sobered after a moment. "You said that you were instructed to meet Solveig and two relic bearers," she said thoughtfully as she stared at her feet. "I take it I'm the second? Oh, and I'm Elena, by the way."

"A pleasure," Solveig replied gravely. "Yes, your sandals make you the second. I confess, I am not sure what Odin has planned for us now…"

"What did the note say?" Liam asked.

Kieth sighed. "More cryptic stuff, I'm afraid. We're to take you to an address and meet with a man there named George. That's all I know; I'd assume he has another note."

"Why would Odin get the two of you involved?" Elena asked. "I mean, I'm still not sure I buy all this, but wouldn't it have been easier to just mail the letters to Liam and I?"

"Why would we have done what they said?" Liam's voice was skeptical. "Still, I'm curious as well. How do you two fit into this? And how do you know all of this stuff?"

Solveig and Kieth exchanged glances. "Without knowing the myths, it is…complicated," she said after a moment. "Suffice to say for now that I am connected with the gods. I assume you are the same?" Kieth nodded.

Elena shook her head. "Okay. I'm going to need some proof of all of this if I'm going to go along with you. Not that I'm not grateful to not be waking up in jail, but still. It seems a bit too convenient that my favorite stories are suddenly real."

Solveig drew her sword in a swift motion and Elena jumped as it burst into flame. "Good Lord," she murmured after taking a moment to regain her composure. "Are you a relic-bearer too?"

It was Kieth who answered, shaking his head as he did so. "No, that sword, that is something else. And if I'm not mistaken…"

Liam was the only one who saw the shadow fall over the window as they spoke. "Get down!" he yelled, diving for Elena as the wall collapsed.

Through the crumbled section of wall came a being similar to the giants Liam had faced in the hospital, but of what he guessed to be a different breed. It was shorter and stockier, its arms almost grotesquely distorted by their muscles. Its skin was the color of dirt and it bore a wild mane of what appeared to be grass. A wooden spear was clutched in its hand, and like the frost giants it was covered in tattoos – though these glowed a sickly green rather than blue. With a roar it threw its weapon, and underneath its raised arm Liam could see dozens more giants.

Kieth moved faster than Liam would have thought possible, lunging from where he had shielded Solveig from the rubble. His hand blocked the spear, knocking it to one side, and Kieth suddenly seemed to fill the room with his presence. "It appears I owe you an apology," he growled to Solveig. "These are indeed Jötun." His eyes seemed to flash red as the giant pounced forward in a tackle. Liam cried out and began to move but was astonished to see the big man hold his ground, suddenly twisting his hips and upper body to throw the giant over his head and *through* the wall behind him.

Solveig looked from Kieth to the newly collapsed wall, a fierce grin upon her face. "Consider it accepted!"

As the other giants bellowed and began to charge, fresh grass appearing in the parking lot where their feet landed, Liam felt a smack to the side of his head.

Care to put my hammer to good use? I didn't give it to you for décor!

Liam grimaced and raised the hammer, preparing to throw it, only to find his line of sight blocked by Kieth. The man let out a blood-curdling howl and charged the army of giants. Solveig let out her bell-like laugh and followed him, trilling as her sword flashed.

"Right. So they're insane," Elena murmured. Liam was not inclined to argue, but he grabbed her hand and pulled her after the duo nonetheless. There was no sense in leaving her unprotected, and he felt it wise to lend his aid in the battle lest he face Thor's wrath.

The world devolved into chaos as he entered the fray, leaving Elena at what he judged a safe distance behind him. He saw glimpses of Solveig skipping through her enemies, and of what he thought was Kieth tackling three of the giants, but overall was too distracted by his own opponents to pay attention to the others. Mjolnir seemed to be guiding his movements and he heard Thor laugh several times. Liam did his best to go with the flow.

It was not until he heard Elena cry out that he thought to look for her, deflecting a hurled boulder as he did so. She was cornered, two giants charging towards her. Liam cast his hammer towards one as he charged the other, praying Mjolnir would return before he entered close combat. He saw it fell one foe, but it was flying back too slowly and he could only watch as the giant swung his axe at Elena in an overhand blow-

Only to find her suddenly ten feet overhead. Liam saw her eyes widen in surprise as the giant bellowed. The cop tackled the beast around the middle and heard the giant roar, but it remained standing. Furious, it whirled around, reaching for Liam. He let go, hand coming back up to catch his hammer. The giant reached for him and Liam prepared to hurl some lightning, hoping the creature wouldn't fall on him.

There was a swift blur of black and the giant suddenly screeched in pain, staggering backwards. Its nose spurted a deep green blood, and Elena laughed as she came to a halt in midair, a small knife held tight in one hand. The giant clutched at its nose, wailing as it lunged for her. Liam quickly swung his hammer, putting the beast out of its misery.

Turning as Elena descended towards him, Liam saw the combat wrapping up. Solveig was just pulling her sword from the corpse of one giant, a faint purple aura surrounding her. Across the way Kieth flung one giant by the arm across the parking lot and through an adjacent wall, roaring as he did so. Liam grimaced at the sight of the big man, liberally coated with the thick green blood of the giants that mingled with some of his own blood. Even from here his red eyes were easy to see, a stark difference from the calm, mild-mannered man whom they'd spoken with minutes before.

Kieth howled as his last enemy remained downed, bellowing his victory to the sky before collapsing. Liam dashed towards him, Solveig close behind as Elena cried out, "No, don't!"

Liam knelt by the man. "Are you alright, mate?"

He jumped backwards as the man lunged for him. Elena swooped in and caught Liam's arm, pulling him up with her into the air. Liam gasped, for there was little trace of anything human left on the man's face. Both tensed as he turned to Solveig.

The woman faced him calmly, and Liam held Elena back as she tried to move towards her. "Leave it," he breathed. "She knows what she's doing."

Kieth growled at the blonde, one foot dragging against the ground in a manner reminiscent of a bull. With a bellow he charged her and Elena gasped, but Solveig merely sidestepped and extended a foot. Kieth crashed into the ground and struggled to rise. Solveig dropped her weight onto his shoulder, sending him back into the asphalt. The tiny woman somehow held him there as the glow around her intensified. After a brief struggle he lay still, panting, and she nodded in satisfaction. Solveig glanced up and saw Liam and Elena staring at her in shock, still hovering in midair.

"You can come down now," she called, obviously amused. They descended, Liam fighting his disbelief at the seemingly solid air beneath their feet. Around them the giants were starting to change shape, dissolving into trees and bushes until the parking lot resembled a small forest. Liam grimaced, wondering how they were going to explain this and hoping that they could get away without needing to.

The purple light slowly faded from around Solveig as she released some of the pressure on Kieth's shoulder. After several minutes his breathing was back under control and he rolled over, the woman moving to allow it. His eyes were squeezed shut, and Liam was relieved to see them back to their normal violet shade as he opened them.

He looked around dazedly. Solveig's eyes were filled with pity as she knelt beside him. "Dear God," he murmured after a moment, looking sickened. "What have I done?"

She squeezed his shoulder, but it was Liam who answered. "Saved our lives, I think."

Kieth breathed a laugh and looked around, blinking at the forest that now surrounded them and flinching at the blood that coated he and Solveig. "Did I- is anyone hurt?"

"Besides you?" Elena replied. That drew a chuckle from him, though he frowned with pain as he laughed. Warily he stood, his balance wavering. Solveig hurried to lend him her support, ducking beneath one of his arms. He flinched at her touch but did not argue. "How do we get out of here?" Elena asked.

"I've a motorcycle, but I don't think I can drive just now," Kieth said, groaning as he shifted.

"I can," Liam replied, glad to be able to repay the big man for what he had done. Kieth fumbled in his pocket for a moment before tossing Liam the keys, nodding towards the bike parked at the end of the row. "Solveig, can you take him on Gunnar?" he continued.

She nodded and whistled for her mount as Elena followed Liam. "I guess I'm with you, then," she said as he mounted the bike.

"It would seem that way," he said with a smile. Liam inserted the keys and turned them, grinning as the engine roared to life. "Where do we meet?" he called to Solveig.

"I do not know the area," she replied as Gunnar came into view.

"Try Prospect Park, it's only a few miles away," Elena offered. "It's pretty secluded."

Solveig nodded. "We shall meet there. Go on, we are faster."

Liam hesitated as Kieth stared at Gunnar, his eyes wide with shock as the horse pranced up to him. The cop looked at Solveig worriedly as she tensed, but Kieth's words took them all by surprise.

"He's magnificent!" the man exclaimed, reaching up a hand for Gunnar to smell. The horse obliged and nuzzled his hand as Solveig blinked in surprise. "A descendant of Sleipnir, am I right?"

"I-yes," she replied, her voice tentative. "I confess, you're the first to recognize him for what he is."

Kieth shook his head, rubbing Gunnar's neck. "He is a king among horses, and you – you ride him. You must be a very special woman indeed."

Solveig actually blushed, and Liam hid his laugh behind a cough as he gestured for Elena to get on behind him. It seemed that even Solveig was not immune to flattery. "You'll have to guide me," he called to Elena as she slipped her arms around his waist.

"Not a problem," she replied as he pulled out of the parking lot, dodging several trees to do so.

Solveig braced Kieth against Gunnar as she mounted and settled herself before extending her hand. He took it and she hauled him up in front of her, murmuring a soft apology as he grimaced. She waited until he was moderately comfortable and then kneed her horse. Gunnar began a trot that quickly picked up pace into a gallop as they reached the road, the horse expertly dodging traffic. Kieth closed his eyes, thinking he preferred not to see his death approaching in the oncoming cars. The least the horse could do would be to ride on the right side of the road – though Solveig *had* said she'd come from London. Perhaps that explained it.

"Damn!" Solveig suddenly groaned, realizing what they had left behind. "That was my best suit of mail!"

Kieth was glad for the distraction. "If we live through whatever is planned for us, I'll make you another."

"Truly?" she asked. "You are a blacksmith?"

He nodded, leaning more heavily into her. "Just finished my apprenticeship at the Ren Faire."

"A rare skill in these times. Did you know your master, or did you travel to find him?"

There was no answer, the big man having dropped off into unconsciousness. Solveig tightened her grip on him, praying that the blood that coated him was mostly that of his enemies.

It took Liam and Elena the better part of half an hour to reach Prospect Park, the traffic having slowed them considerably. They found Solveig and Kieth waiting near the main entrance. Solveig bore a bag filled with what looked to be medical supplies. She shrugged as Liam raised an eyebrow in surprise. "I left cash," she explained.

He shook his head but said nothing, remembering how well their last hospital trip had turned out. "Where to now?" he asked.

"There's a couple of secluded areas by the lake and Terrace Bridge," Elena said. Seeing their blank looks, she pointed. "That way."

They followed her directions, Liam taking the motorcycle as far as the road would allow before parking it. He and Elena walked alongside Gunnar the rest of the way.

Finally they came to a forested area that Solveig judged suitable. She handed Kieth down to Liam, who grunted but managed to keep the big man from faceplanting on the ground. Solveig dismounted gratefully, sending Gunnar off a little ways to graze as she helped Liam set Kieth with his back to a tree. The ground here was covered in a light frost, but no snow had fallen on it thanks to the heavy covering of trees.

Kieth moaned and began to stir as Solveig knelt next to him, digging through her bag. Elena joined her, fighting a laugh as she saw the amount of painkillers the woman had grabbed.

"I am unfamiliar with your medicines," she confessed as Liam walked the perimeter, making sure that there was no one around to see them. Elena began to sort the items in order of usefulness, explaining them to Solveig as she went. Liam came back into hearing range just as she was saying, "So you see, he can't take more than two or three of any of these because there's too much acetaminophen in them. Too many could kill him…although with his body mass, we might be able to get away with four."

"Med student?" Liam asked.

"Librarian, actually," she replied with a quick smile.

"How does a librarian know so much about medicine and myths?"

She shrugged. "I told you, I like to read. Get his shirt off for me, would you?"

Liam blinked but complied, walking over to where the man lay. He decided that at this point it would be easiest to cut it off – the shirt was already in tatters. "And the stealing? Where does that come in?"

Solveig saw Elena tense as she pulled out rubbing alcohol and an antibiotic. It took her a moment to answer, and when she did her voice was terse. "That's personal."

He glanced at her, taking the bottle of rubbing alcohol she offered. "You broke the law, and I'm a cop. It's kind of my job to ask."

She grimaced as Solveig tossed him a cloth. "I needed the money, alright? Stick me in jail after all of this is done if you have to."

Liam shook his head, beginning to wipe Kieth's wounds. The man hissed and opened his eyes, grimacing as his cuts began to burn. "Here, let me," Solveig said, stepping in. Liam handed the cloth to her and walked over to where Elena was still sitting, crouching beside her.

"Sorry," he offered after a moment as she ignored him. "You just don't strike me as a criminal. You walked past a lot of jewels – what were you looking for? The shoes?"

She looked down, suddenly fighting a smile. "A ladder, actually. I just got distracted and wanted to see what the patterns on the sandals were."

Liam blinked. "A ladder. Right. I'm sure that would go for an awful lot on the black market."

She laughed, and after a moment Liam joined her. He might not understand her reasons, and he couldn't approve of what she'd been trying to do, but she was infectiously positive no matter the situation. "Alright, have it your way," he said after taking a moment to sober. "You caught on to using the shoes pretty quick, though."

Elena shrugged. "The first time was just luck as I tried to dive out of the way. After that it wasn't too hard – there's only so many relics they could be, and I was already in the air."

Across from them, Kieth hissed as Solveig dabbed a particularly deep cut. "Forgive me," she murmured, her hair hiding her face as the others talked.

"My own fault," he replied, and his voice was remorseful. "I should have controlled myself better."

She glanced at him in surprise. "What do you mean?"

"I gave in to my rage. I could have killed all of you without knowing it. A few scrapes and cuts are easily borne."

Solveig shook her head, touching his shoulder. She considered her words for a moment before speaking. "We are what we are. There is no shame in your heritage, just as there is none in mine. We may not always like our circumstances, but there is a purpose to them. You shouldn't punish yourself for saving our lives."

He looked up at her. "And what if I hadn't been able to regain control?"

She shrugged. "We will never know. For now, I know that you saved us – and for that, you have my thanks."

He blinked, and she was surprised to see tears in the big man's eyes. "I-thank you. Your words mean much to me."

Elena glanced up from across the way, cutting in. "You're a berserk, aren't you?"

"What's a berserk?" Liam asked as Kieth looked away.

"It's from the Norse words 'sark' and 'bear', meaning 'clothed in bear skin'. The berserk were followers of Odin in Midgard. It's where we get the word 'berserker'," Elena replied.

Liam's eyes widened as Kieth nodded. "My ancestors were berserk. Every now and then one of our family inherits the traits."

"So is this a once a month thing, or what?" the cop asked.

Kieth gave a bitter laugh. "Not quite. More like the Hulk. If I get mad, I go berserk. I've worked for as long as I can remember trying to control it, but it's hard."

Elena cocked her head to one side, curious. "So did you have rageful temper tantrums when you were a baby or what?"

He chuckled. "No, thankfully for my parents. It didn't hit me until about puberty – the same with you, I'd imagine," he added with a glance to Solveig.

She nodded, continuing to bind his wounds as the others looked at her. "Are you a berserk too?" Liam asked.

"No," she replied. "I am what is called a Lifkyr." Kieth nodded as she continued, "A descendant of a mortal and a Valkyrie."

"I thought they were a myth!" Elena exclaimed. Solveig shot her an amused look, glancing down at herself and then back up as if to say, *Obviously not.*

"You seem to be fond of stories," she said with a chuckle as Elena blushed. "Let me tell you mine."

"Many centuries ago there lived a Valkyrie named Brynhildr. The Valkyr were the angels of the battlefield, fearsome women warriors who could sense the approach of death and were tasked by Odin to aid his chosen side in battle. When a warrior died they bore him up to the Halls of Valhalla, the Hall of the Slain, where he would join the ranks of the Einherjar. There he would be waited upon by the Valkyr and never know sorrow until the day of the Ragnarök."

"Brynhildr, however, had disobeyed Odin's command and allowed the wrong side to win. For this, she was condemned to marry the first mortal she saw. She begged Odin for mercy and eventually softened his heart; he agreed to lay her sleeping in a castle called Hindfell, hidden behind a wall of flame. There she knew that only the truly brave would travel – and if no one came, she would lie sleeping for all eternity."

"So basically she was Sleeping Beauty?" Liam asked. "Would that make Odin the evil queen?"

Solveig glared at him and he quieted, though the others snickered. "There are similarities, yes. Your culture has stolen much from the Norse. May I continue?" She waited a moment and then spoke on.

"Eventually a man named Sigurðr came over the wall on his horse, a descendant of Sleipnir and an ancestor of Gunnar. He had been on many adventures of his own prior to this, including the reforging of a magical sword named Gram." Here Solveig patted her own blade.

Kieth nodded. "I called that one."

She smiled at him before continuing her tale. "Sigurðr had also slain a mighty dragon and in the process acquired a cursed ring. He bore this ring when he entered the castle and met Brynhildr, which of course doomed their relationship from the start. Sigurðr awoke her and they swore to be wed. That night they swapped stories of their lives, sharing all – including Sigurðr's only vulnerability. He then gave her the cursed ring as a sign of his love and left in the morning, vowing to return."

"He didn't know it was cursed," Elena interjected, seeing the look on Liam's face.

"Indeed. Their actions had far-reaching consequences - from their union sprang my ancestors, the descendants of a human and a Valkyr. There are a few other family lines around the world, but not many. Any male born to the line has the potential to be a great warrior if he should so choose; any woman born is given a greater choice still."

Here she looked down, and her far-off tone told the others she had given this a great deal of thought. "When we enter our teens we are given a few basic abilities – the knowledge of how to wield any weapon, increased strength, slowed aging, and the ability to fly. The more we use our powers the greater they become – the less we use them, the quicker they fade. We are marked with the sign of the Valkyr when these things are gifted, and this mark informs us of how much or little we have used."

Solveig lifted her sheet of hair and twisted, revealing a purple tattoo of two wings on her back. Liam blinked. "That purple light around you when you fight," he asked. "Is that when you're using your powers?"

She nodded. "However, we cannot have the best of both worlds. Eventually we are forced to make a choice – either give up our powers entirely, or embrace them and become a Valkyr."

"Was Gunnar a part of the deal?" Elena asked.

Solveig smiled, the expression fleeting but sincere. "No, he was a gift to me on my tenth birthday, before I received my powers. I do not know if he was a gift from Odin or from one of my ancestors, but he has been my faithful companion ever since.

Liam blinked. "How old are you, exactly?"

Kieth swatted him on the arm and Liam blushed, realizing that the question was rude, but Solveig answered without seeming to care. "I am twenty-six."

"You're joking," Elena gasped. "You look way younger! How long does your kind live?"

Solveig shrugged. "It varies depending on what life path we choose. My mother was forty-seven when she chose a mortal life."

"What about the sword?" Kieth asked after a moment of silence. "Where did you get Gram?"

"A family heirloom, passed down through generations. My mother gifted it to me before I left."

Liam frowned, considering. "What happened to Brynhildr and Sigurðr? You said something about them being doomed?"

"There was tragedy, of course," she replied. "They made an opera of it several years ago."

Kieth took over. "Sigurðr was delayed in his returning by several months and wound up staying in a castle owned by a wicked queen. She fed him a potion that made him fall in love with her daughter, and he forgot about Brynhildr entirely. He married the daughter, and perhaps all would have been well for them if his bride's brother had not heard of a maiden who dwelled behind a curtain of fire…"

Kieth trailed off as the others stared at him. "I'm a fan of the opera," he offered as an explanation. They laughed, though Solveig looked at him thoughtfully as he continued. "Anyway, the brother convinces Sigurðr to go with him and try to rescue the maiden, and it turns out that Sigurðr's horse Grani is the only one who can jump the fire. The horse, of course, won't bear the brother, so Sigurðr puts on the brother's armor and goes in his stead. He tells Brynhildr that he's the brother – it's funny, but his name was Gunnar too, now that I think of it."

Solveig nodded, continuing the tale. "Brynhildr thinks that she recognizes him but he refuses to take off his armor until they're over the wall again. She says that they have to stay the night because she is tired, and since she will not be swayed, he agrees. In the morning he wakes up first and sees her ring. No one is sure if he remembered something about it or simply acted on impulse, but Sigurðr takes the ring and pockets it."

"Afterwards they jump over the wall of fire; Gunnar and Sigurðr change armor out of sight," Kieth added. "Gunnar walks up and makes a big deal of removing his helmet. They head back to the castle, and by the end of the ride Brynhildr is half convinced that Sigurðr was just a dream. She marries Gunnar and all is well for a while until Sigurðr's wife hears the tale. She begs him for the ring he took, and he reluctantly gives it to her."

"Eventually she and Brynhildr wind up bickering about something, and they begin to boast about their respective husbands…'My husband is braver than yours', and so on. Finally Brynhildr says something about how no mortal but Gunnar would dare to cross the flames that imprisoned her. Sigurðr's wife, of course, says that he didn't – that it was Sigurðr who did, and oh, here's the ring to prove it."

Liam grimaced, imagining the scene as Solveig finished the tale. "Needless to say, Brynhildr was furious. She demanded that Gunnar kill Sigurðr and tells him of his vulnerable spot, but he is too good of a man and refuses to murder his brother-in-law. His brothers, however, have no such morals and ambush Sigurðr, stabbing him in the back and killing him."

"Gunnar orders that Sigurðr's funeral be huge. Brynhildr watches from the battlements, and just as Sigurðr's pyre is set alight, she leaps to join him, crying out for him to wait so that they might rise together to Valhalla."

In the silence that followed Liam fought to regain his composure, coughing thickly before asking, "That's it? What is it with people and tragedies?"

"Mythology – the original soap opera," Elena added with a grin.

Kieth, however, shook his head. "It doesn't end there. It is said that after the pyre was burnt out, Grani was found missing from the stables. And when the stablehands were questioned, one admitted to seeing a horse galloping into the sky – a horse with two riders upon its back."

Elena shook her head. "That is a *much* better ending."

Solveig laughed. "Indeed it is."

Liam let out a low whistle. "Well, way to make me feel normal, you two. All I've got is a magic hammer – you two actually *are* magic!"

A borrowed *magic hammer at that,* Thor chimed in.

The others chuckled. "Back to matters at hand; did I hear you say that you know what your sandals are?" Solveig asked Elena.

The younger woman nodded. "Really, there's only so many myths with magical shoes, and you implied that these were Loki's. Given what they do, I think it's likely that they're the shoes he stole from Brokkr and Sindri."

Liam was relieved to see that his blank look was shared by Kieth and Solveig. Elena sighed and continued, "The two dwarf smiths that Loki made a wager with? He stole a pair of sandals from their forge that gave him the ability to run on the sea or on the sky. Most versions of the myths don't contain it, but some do. The shoes don't have a name that I know of – although if we mix mythologies, I guess they could be the sandals of Hermes…"

"*No.*" Kieth and Solveig glanced at each other, the lifkyr gesturing for Kieth to explain. "You don't mix the pantheons. They're not…overly fond of one another."

Elena blinked. "You mean Hermes actually- I was only joking!"

Solveig shook her head. "It is best to not. But you said that you had dreamt of Loki…this is not good."

Kieth added, "You probably already know, but I wouldn't take any advice from him."

Elena laughed. "Advice from the god of mischief – yeah, that sounds smart. I hadn't planned on it, don't worry."

"All the same, it is worrisome that one of his artifacts – especially so powerful of one – should be found now. Be on your guard."

Liam frowned and cut in. "You said earlier that Baldr's death meant that the Ragnarök had come – what does that mean?"

They all looked at him. "Do you know *nothing* about Norse mythology?" Elena asked in surprise.

"He knows the comics," Solveig explained with a wry grin.

Liam rolled his eyes. "I was always more interested in Greek mythology. Assume that I know nothing."

"Oh, we will," Kieth said, his grin wicked. Liam shot him a dirty look and the big man closed his eyes in mock pain, gesturing to his wounds.

Elena bit back a laugh as she continued. "The Ragnarök literally means the end of the world as we know it. From the Norse 'ragna', meaning god, and 'rök', meaning end. When it comes most of the gods will die. Yggdrasill – the World Tree," she added, seeing the look on Liam's face. When his confusion remained, she sighed. "The tree that holds all the realms – planets - together; think of it as space. It will be mostly destroyed in fire, along with all of the worlds."

Liam thought for a moment. "At Baldr's funeral, Odin said something… something about the end having begun. Do you think that had something to do with this Ragnarök?"

Are my whiskers worthy of worship? Wait. It's rhetorical. Don't answer.

Liam's hand jumped to his face at the words, and he silently cursed the god as he felt the beard that he had so painstakingly shaven last night, now grown back in all of its former 'glory'. He missed what Solveig was saying, coming back to the real world only when Elena waved her hand in front of his face.

"Sorry," he muttered as Thor laughed. "Just being annoyed."

"He keeps trying to get rid of the beard," Solveig murmured to Kieth, who laughed. "As I was saying, this is important. If Odin mentioned the Ragnarök in your presence, it is likely he knew you were listening. What exactly did he say?"

Liam thought back. "Something about the end being near. He told Thor that he knew what he had to do – Thor was thinking about some counsels they'd had about what to do. And then – it was weird. I think he was talking to me; he told me that I too had a part to play."

Kieth and Solveig exchanged dark looks as Elena rocked back on her heels. "It's not uncommon for Odin to gather warriors on Earth," she said after a moment. "But usually he's more subtle about it. A disguise, at the very least!"

"Subtle might not be the right word," Kieth interjected, "Since he normally disappears while the hero is watching and seems to always wear the same outfit."

The lifkyr frowned and turned to Elena. "I think that I remember something important about the Ragnarök, but I feel you would have a better knowledge of this than I. Tell me, what events do the legends say shall lead up to the fateful day?"

The librarian bit her lip as she thought. "Midgard is supposed to be the first to notice. We'll experience a worldwide war."

"Which one?" Liam asked.

She shrugged. "It's supposed to be a three year war, and both of the World Wars were too long for that. I suppose they might have only counted when everyone was involved – I don't know how the gods see these things. But after that we're supposed to have a Fimbul winter, full of blizzards and freezes."

Everyone looked to the ground, where frost was clearly fighting a winning battle against the grass. Solveig nodded. "It is as I feared."

"It's been about the same in Arizona," Liam murmured.

Kieth shivered. "What else?"

"The wolves will swallow the sun and moon – don't ask," she said to Liam, who closed his mouth. "The stars will fall from the sky, and the very earth itself shall shake. Then all the really bad stuff starts happening."

"It gets worse?" Liam asked.

"Very," Solveig replied as Elena nodded. "We need to get to that address right away," the lifkyr added as she stood. She glanced at Kieth. "Can you ride?"

He grimaced, but nodded. "Just give me some of those painkillers first. Good Lord, woman, do you think you got enough?"

She blushed but faced him defiantly. "I was not sure how many you would require."

Kieth chuckled and held out a hand, catching the bottle that Liam chucked him. He carefully shook out three pills, knocking them back without water. He tucked the bottle into his pocket and only then looked down at his freshly bandaged chest. The white stood out in stark contrast to his dark skin and he laughed. "I don't suppose anyone has a spare shirt?"

Liam shrugged off his jacket and tossed it to him. "I'm off duty, so technically speaking I shouldn't be wearing it either."

Kieth pulled it on, wincing as the too-small shirt pinched his arms. "I've always wanted to be a cop." They helped him to rise, relieved to find his good humor remained. Though he staggered upon first standing, he was able to walk unaided after a moment. "I'll take my keys back now, thank you," he nodded to Liam.

"You're sure you can drive?" he asked, waiting for the big man's nod before he tossed him the keys. "Alright then. But I'm not taking the horse – no offense," he said to Gunnar, who blinked innocently at them from where he grazed.

"I'll go," Elena volunteered, and the lifkyr nodded at her.

"You're stuck with me then, Liam," Kieth said. "But can I hitch a ride back to my bike?"

He and Solveig mounted up and Gunnar bounded off towards the parking lot. Elena and Liam grabbed the remaining medical supplies and stuffed them back in the bag before beginning their walk.

"So, you're a Christian?" she asked after a bit.

"I- yes. How did you know?"

She laughed at him. "You're wearing a cross, genius."

Liam reached up – sure enough, his necklace had fallen out of his shirt. "Are you?"

"Catholic." She shrugged. "You're taking all this talk of gods rather well."

He chuckled, remembering his initial reaction. "Solveig told me to think of them as aliens. It's working pretty well so far. What about you?"

She shrugged again. "I grew up with the stories. I don't think of them as being gods like my God, though I've never heard them described as aliens before. It's weird, and I'll probably freak out about it later, but for now, it's just like being in one of my stories."

"I do read, you know," he said after a pause. "Just not necessarily mythology."

She laughed. "I didn't think you were illiterate, don't worry. I can totally see you curling up with a romance novel."

Liam snorted but didn't deny it. "What got you into mythology?"

Elena smiled. "My dad. He was a librarian too – kind of started me on the path at a young age. Myths were always his favorite stories. I honestly prefer Greek, but Norse was one of the first mythologies I read."

Please. Why would anyone prefer Zeus to me? I'm obviously far superior. And better looking.

Liam laughed, explaining at her puzzled look, "Thor says he's way better than Zeus."

She laughed. "Good to know he has a sense of humor. Though I do have to wonder…what all other pantheons might be real?"

By now they were within sight of the others. Solveig rode up next to them and gestured for Elena to mount up as Kieth revved his bike. Liam gestured for him to wait a minute and knelt by Gunnar, his hands cupped. He winked at Elena as she looked at him in surprise. "Guess I read too many of those romance novels."

She blushed but stepped into his hand as Solveig rolled her eyes. Liam vaulted Elena into her seat, realizing as he did so that the novels made it sound *much* easier than it actually was. Once she was situated he headed for the bike, swinging up behind Kieth. "You should really get a helmet," he called, and the man laughed.

"Had one. Left it behind when the Jötuns attacked, I'm afraid. Do you know the address?" he called to Solveig.

She nodded. "But perhaps it's best if we stay close. If matters are truly as grave as we fear…"

The big man shuddered and nodded, seeing the world burning in his mind. They took off, Gunnar seeming to pout at the relatively slow pace of the bike.

It took many hours traveling at breakneck speeds along the highways to reach the address. Along the way Liam had uttered many prayers that improved reflexes were among a berserk's abilities. He had almost decided that he preferred to travel by horse, a thought that made Thor laugh. Still, at least Kieth rode on the right side of the road.

"Wow," said Elena as Kieth killed the engine. "I don't know what I was expecting, but it definitely wasn't this."

The mansion stood near the border to Canada, several miles outside of Rochester. It was surrounded by greenery and a frozen lake, nature and the man-made structure co-existing without fuss. It was huge and secluded with only a dirt road leading up to it. Its cast iron gates were flung wide, and the house itself had all of the lights turned on. Though only somewhere around five in the evening, the sun was already beginning to set – strange for the middle of summer. Elena shot a puzzled glance towards the sky and gasped, causing the others to look up as well.

"What in the world is that?" Liam asked in shock. The rapidly descending sun seemed to be being chased by a streak of black cloud.

"Sköll," Solveig murmured. "The wolves have sped up their chase."

"We should hurry," Kieth said, his wounds making him walk stiffly as he headed for the door. The others followed him, still shooting worried glances at the sky.

Whereas the mansion in town had seemed to exist solely to stand out from its surroundings, this one seemed focused on blending in. It was made of solid logs of oak that blended nicely with the forest background, and its pillars, rather than being made of marble, were of a tasteful red wood. The window frames and door were made of the same material, and next to the door there hung an old fashioned bell. Solveig stepped up and rang it sharply, the clear tone echoing around the porch. Elena smiled at a nearby rocking chair draped with a quilt, a book laying nearby. Someone had clearly been enjoying the scenery.

The door opened moments after the bell had run out, and whatever Liam had expected to find, it wasn't this. "Come in, come in!" the old man exclaimed as he flung open the door. "I've been waiting for you!"

He sat in a motorized wheelchair, and judging from the marks on the floor he used it often. There was a sparkle in his blue eyes as he peered at them over the top of spectacles, and what little white, downy hair remained on his balding head matched the fluff that grew in a well kept beard. He smiled up at them, examining them as they eyed him, and finally uttered a laugh.

"Well," he said after a moment. "I must say that you're not what I imagined – though I'm sure you could say the same of me. Solveig, I'd guess?" he asked with a glance at her. She nodded, surprised, and he smiled. "And Kieth – my good man, do come sit down, you look exhausted. I'll see if I can't find you a shirt that fits a *little* better."

Kieth laughed and nodded his thanks, following the man as he wheeled around. The others trailed after, admiring the decorations. It was obvious that the house had once been a hunting lodge, but the taxidermy displays that had once lined the walls had now given way to an eclectic mix of items that transformed it into a home. Every now and then a glassy-eyed head could still be seen on the wall, but for the most part it was covered in pictures and statues – and, most of all, bookcases.

They rounded a corner and entered a cozy living room. Couches and cushy armchairs were spread at seemingly random intervals, and a crackling fire burned in the hearth. Kieth sank gratefully onto one of the couches as the old man headed to a cedar chest pushed against one wall, opening it and pulling out a plaid flannel shirt. He tossed it to Kieth. "Try that on."

The man shrugged gingerly out of Liam's shirt and pulled on the red flannel, grinning as he was able to close and button it without difficulty. "Thank you very much, sir."

He grinned. "Call me George. And you, young man, what's your name?"

Liam turned from his observation of a weapon display above the fireplace, spears and swords positioned on hooks in the wall. "Liam, sir. You've a lovely home."

"Oh, yes!" Elena added, turning from her perusal of a bookcase. "Your collection is amazing!"

He laughed. "Thank you, miss – I've had a lifetime to add to it. And you are?"

"Elena, sir."

"Elena, eh? Not Elena Hernandez?"

Her eyes widened. "George MacDonald? I thought I recognized you!"

He chuckled again as the others looked on. "Indeed you did! It's been years, lassie! How's your father? I heard about his recent battle."

She looked down. "Well enough, sir. The chemo seems to be helping."

Liam looked at her in shock. He knew how expensive chemo-therapy could be, and she'd said she needed the money – was it possible she'd been stealing to support her father's battle with cancer?

The man nodded sadly. "Well, if there's ever anything I can do for you or yours, please let me know. But you didn't come here for such matters, I daresay. Onward to business? Oh, do everyone sit down and let me ring us up some tea. You look ready to drop."

The others sank gratefully into the eclectic mix of seating arrangements. An honest-to-goodness butler appeared in the doorway and George said a few words to him before rolling over and parking himself so that they formed a circle. "Now then. Where do we begin? I assume you know why you're here."

They shook their heads. "My letter said to bring the others here," Kieth said. "We don't know why – though at a guess, I'd say it has to do with the Ragnarök."

George nodded thoughtfully. "Well, judging from the looks of you I'd say your story is more interesting than mine. Why don't you tell it to me and we'll see if we can't fit together the pieces?"

After a moment they began to tell their tale, George listening with interest and asking small questions in the pauses that reminded them of details they had forgotten. When they had finished he contemplated them for a moment before nodding quietly.

"Well," George said, "It appears you've had quite the adventure; my own tale is dull by comparison, I'm afraid. I received no letter, though the sender of them did appear to me in a dream last night. He told me that today I would receive visitors, and named two of you. He instructed me to open my library to you and to impart all of my knowledge of the Ragnarök and of the Norns to you, as well as the history of the relic bearers – and, of course, to provide you with a safe place to stay for as long as you require it."

"Why would Odin want you to tell us of the Norns?" Solveig asked.

"What are they, anyway?" Liam interjected.

George shrugged as his butler walked in with a tray of sandwiches and a pot of hot tea.

"Thank you, Tom," George said with a smile. The man returned it and left, and they continued their conversation with refreshments. "I'm not sure why he would wish me to tell you of the Wyrd sisters, but I'm sure he has his reasons. As to what they are – are you familiar with Greek mythology?"

Liam nodded. "To some degree. Moreso than I am with Norse."

The old man smiled. "Most people are. The Norns are similar to the Greek Fates, in that they are three sisters who measure the thread of time. There are some differences, and that is not their only job; but if you are correct and the Ragnarök is indeed approaching, perhaps it would be best to focus on that."

"We know some of the Ragnarök – the events leading up to it, mostly, and that it is the end of the universe," Solveig said. "What Kieth and I did not know, Elena did – but did Odin offer you no clues as to why we needed to know all of this?"

George shook his head. "Only that it would be needed before the end… which is a loaded sentence, considering the topic."

"Well, it is not as though we can stop the Ragnarök – is it?" Solveig trailed off as the others looked at her, Elena and Kieth both fighting back yawns.

"For now, my dear, I think you all need some sleep," George said after a moment. "You look positively weary, and from what you've told me you've had little in the way of rest. These matters are better mused upon in the morning."

"But if Odin said that we needed to know this-"

"He also said that you should rest for as long as you required it. So sleep, my dear; there will be time enough later for talk." He waited until she had nodded her agreement to continue. "There's plenty of space here, if you would like, or bedrooms down the hall. Bathroom is through that door and to the right; please make yourselves at home and feel free to bathe. For now, I'll be in my study trying to refresh my memory on all of these subjects. If you need me, don't hesitate to call."

He wheeled out of the room with a smile and the four exchanged looks. "Shower," Liam and Elena said at the same time, trading a laugh afterward.

"Sleep for me," Kieth said, obviously exhausted. "Painkillers always knock me out." He leaned back, wincing as he pulled his legs up onto the couch.

Solveig nodded her agreement. "Better to sleep while we can." She leaned her sword in the corner behind her and tucked her legs up under her, curling up in the chair like a cat. "But you two may do as you wish."

Liam gestured for Elena to take the first bath, but she shook her head. "I want to soak – you go ahead. You'll probably be done faster."

He sighed. "There go my hopes of a bubble bath, but all right." She laughed as he walked by.

As he stepped past the door to the study, George called out, "Fresh clothes in the chest, if you'd like."

Turning, Liam headed back and dug through the chest until he found some clothes that were the right size. Elena grinned at him as he headed for the shower.

Liam emerged from his shower refreshed and cleanly shaven. He shook his head, amused at Thor's grumbling, and stopped in the doorway to the study as he saw George and Tom murmuring back and forth. Tom left with a small smile after a moment and George turned to Liam with a grin of greeting.

"Don't mind Tom, he's rather shy," he said. "The lad's the only family I've got here, another minor relic bearer like me."

"You're a relic bearer?" Elena asked in surprise as she appeared at the doorway, a bundle of clean clothes held under one arm.

"I am indeed; but perhaps the tale is better told when all can hear it. For now, let it suffice to say that I have some idea of what the two of you are going through." He winked at them, and the duo laughed.

"Well, my turn," Elena said. "Thank you, George, and goodnight."

He smiled as she walked past, Liam's gaze following her. He turned back to the man and found George eyeing him with a piercing gaze. "Her father," Liam asked tentatively. "Cancer?"

George nodded. "I don't know the particulars, but yes. An old colleague of mine from the library, in case you're wondering."

Liam nodded, thinking for a minute before looking back at George. "I wonder – you said we could use your study. Do you have any books that are a basic introduction to Norse mythology?"

The man raised his eyebrows. "Don't you want to sleep?"

Liam shrugged. "I'm used to long hours. Besides, I keep slowing us down by not knowing the legends."

George's eyes twinkled. "And this has nothing to do with the young lady knowing more than you."

He flushed. "No, nothing like that. I just don't want to seem stupid." His blush deepened as the older man gave him a knowing nod.

"Alright, then. Through that door-" he pointed through a small door behind his desk, flanked on both sides by bookshelves, "- is my collection of less…scholarly books. They'll give you the basic rundown without any of the debates you'll find in these."

Liam looked down at George's desk, which was spread liberally with books and papers covered in a thin, angular writing. "I take it yours are slightly heavier reads."

George chuckled. "They assume that you know all about Norse mythology and get down to the nitty-gritty details – which, while quite enjoyable for me, would be a nightmare for you. First shelf on your right once you walk in – let me know if you have any questions."

"Thank you," the cop replied as he walked past. Within the room he found little floor space – there was one window facing east, beside which rested a cozy armchair that had obviously seen much use. The walls of the room were hidden behind bookshelves, which were filled to overflowing. Though Liam was sure they were organized somehow, he couldn't for the life of him see how.

"Sorry for the mess," George called, and Liam laughed. Turning to his right he eyed the first bookshelf he saw. The majority of it was occupied by books covered with depictions of the Norse pantheon. He ran his hand along them, curious, until one caught his eye.

Pulling it off of the shelf, Liam eyed the picture. It was familiar, and uncannily true to what he had seen. A large boat upon which stood a burning pyre took up the majority of the cover – the rest of it was filled with a motley crew, at the forefront of which stood a man easily recognized as Odin. His eye was a bright blue that seemed to stare into Liam even from the pages.

Liam settled into the armchair and began to read.

Tyrsday

Tonight I saw my life as it might be – a powerful life. So, so powerful; there is nothing that I cannot do. But something goes terribly wrong. I grow too strong and my enemies use those that I love to get to me. Though I defeat them, my life lies in shambles and my loved ones lie dead. I am dragged kicking and screaming to the gates of Valhalla, my choice made for me…

He emerged six hours later, having gone through two books besides his first. Inside the study he found George, who sat at his desk poring over an old manuscript. The old man looked up and smiled at him. "Finished already?"

Liam laughed. "No, but I wanted to sleep. Although, there was *one* question that I had."

"Just one?"

"For now, at least. Now, I know that the gods are gods and all that, and being so they're superior to us, as Thor keeps reminding me…but I'm pretty sure that it isn't physically possible for Loki to give birth to a horse."

George snorted. "Most scholars hope that particular myth was mistranslated."

Liam raised an eyebrow. "Most?"

The older man shook his head, still laughing. "There are a few die-hard fanatics who insist that everything was translated properly, along with a few strange theories that Loki is actually a woman. It's all very odd." He paused for a moment, enjoying the look on Liam's face. "But off to bed with you – it's almost two."

"Good night, then; and thank you again, sir," Liam said respectfully, carefully navigating the stacks of books. George waved him out, and Liam wondered how late the man would be up as the old scholar returned to his books.

The others were sprawled out on the couches, all asleep. He paused for a moment by Elena to fix the blanket that had slipped from her shoulders, and though she stirred she did not awaken. He hoped her dreams were more peaceful than his had been of late.

Liam grabbed a reclining armchair close to the embers of the fire and stretched out, his eyes weary from reading. His mind swirled with thoughts of the tales he had seen. As he drifted off he was dimly aware of Thor bidding him good night.

The snake hangs above me, his coils visible to my naked eye. I see in Sigyn's eyes that she will soon have to leave me, and terror fills me. "Don't," I plead. "Please, don't-"

Tears pour down her cheeks as she shakes her head. "I'm sorry, my love," she murmurs, and as she moves her burden I burn in white hot agony.

Time passes – a moment? A day? A year? Lost in time I writhe in pain, screaming until my lungs are hoarse. Finally the basin is held above me once more. It takes a minute for my cries to stop, and when I open my eyes it is only the chains that bind me that prevent me from bolting.

It is not my wife who stands above me – instead I see a burly arm holding the stone basin. It is Thor.

"Loki," I mutter, looking at him with loathing. This trickster has always left a foul taste in my mouth, though recently it has turned bitter. "What do you want her for?"

"Who?" he cries out, his eyes still watering from the torture he has endured.

I growl, my hand tipping slightly, and he cries out in horror. I look on with pleasure as he cringes, the threat of a new deluge of poison too much for him to bear. Gently, I lay my hand level, not even trying to hide my smirk. "Don't play coy with me. Why give her the sandals now?"

His eyes glint with something I cannot fathom – is it mere madness, or something darker? "I assure you, it is mere happenstance that those old things be found now. I've little use for them, just a castoff-"

My free hand comes up to his neck, throttling him, and I wait until he turns red to release him. Well…perhaps I linger for a few moments more than I strictly should. Already I can hear footsteps at the end of the tunnel; Sigyn will soon return.

"Know this, Loki. Should any harm come – to any of them – it shall be your blood that pays the debt."

He smirks at me. "Grown soft for the mortals, Thor? Is your human influencing you?"

Impossible! He cannot know-

I watch his smug smile grow and realize that my own reaction has sealed his knowledge. "Curse you, Loki," I growl. "To the darkest pits of Hel I curse you."

"Where's Mjolnir, Thor? Where is your faithful hammer? Do you really think that you can stop what is coming? Surely not even Odin could be so foolish-"

I have heard enough of his blathering. I turn, tossing the basin to one side. As the venom lands upon his naked skin I hear his cries begin anew. It is to the sound of this that I make my exit, caught up in his words…is the human changing me?

Through the blazing pain, my mind endures. The Æsir do not stand unaided, and Thor's bond with the mortals is stronger than I had expected. All the same, they are shaken…and my plans run deep.

But in the end, even that thought is stripped from me, and I scream once more into the never-ending white hot abyss within which I am trapped...for now.

"Elena. Elena!"

She sat up with a jolt, her eyes wide and her body shaking. The others knelt around her, and Liam gripped her shoulder. She panted, trying to catch her breath, her legs entangled in her blanket.

"Are you alright?" Solveig asked worriedly.

She shook her head, trying to find words and for some reason unable to meet Liam's gaze. He stared at her for a moment longer before rocking back on his heels. "My God," he murmured. "You felt it? I'm so sorry."

Kieth and Solveig looked at him in surprise as Elena shook her head again, still unable to speak. A soft squeaking noise drew their attention to the hallway and they glanced over to find George wheeling swiftly through, a mug of hot tea held in his hands.

"Here you are, my dear," he said as he handed it to her. "My own special blend. It helps me when what I see is too much to bear."

Elena gave a shaky laugh, taking it from him with a nod of thanks. The steam from the cup relaxed her and she inhaled several times before taking a drink.

Solveig looked at Liam. "What do you mean, she could feel it? What happened?"

The cop held up a hand, gazing to one side. "No," he muttered. "No, I don't care! You don't do that again!" There was a pause and the others stared at him. George shook his head at Solveig as she started to repeat her question. "Because she could feel it, idiot! And I will *not* have you torturing my friend!"

"He looks almost in a rage," Kieth murmured to Solveig, who nodded slowly. The look on Liam's face was one of fierce protectiveness, and she wondered what had sparked this new emotion.

After a moment Liam looked up again. "Sorry about that, just straightening some things out."

"What happened?" Kieth asked calmly.

"Thor paid Loki a visit," Liam replied. "It wasn't pretty."

Elena shook her head, the tea already clearing it. "Thank you," she murmured to George before turning to the rest of the group. "It gets worse, I'm afraid. Loki isn't worried – he's got something planned."

George looked between the two of them. "You shared this dream?"

"From opposite perspectives," Liam replied. "Thor wanted to know why Loki had picked Elena, and why now. He knows he's planning something, but he can't figure out what."

"And Loki – I can't even see what he's got planned. I think he knows I'm watching so he's hiding it, but he kept thinking about escaping somehow."

"What did Thor mean by picked?" Liam asked. "Elena just found the sandals. It's not like they were sent to her or anything, right?"

George sighed, sinking back into his chair. "It appears it's time for a brief history of the relic bearers. A bearer is not merely someone who has found a relic – it is someone who has found a relic that works for them. There have been many who have founds relics that were, to them, merely fragments of something ancient. Several have been left in museums for centuries, waiting for the right person to gain hold of them."

"Most scholars among the relic bearers believe that a relic will only choose someone similar to the god that once possessed it. I myself bear a relic of Odin – whose relics traditionally go to those who have sacrificed something for the greater good and learned from said sacrifice in keeping with the god himself. Those who receive Thor's relics are traditionally brave warriors in their own field, and tend to be headstrong and stubborn."

"All three," Elena murmured, and Liam shot her a tentative grin.

"Quite. Loki's bearers tend to have a bit of a penchant for mischief, or for hiding in the shadows. Many turn out to be petty criminals. As you can tell, this is not always the case, but it does seem to apply to the majority. Heimdallr's bearers tend to find those who keep watch over others, guarding them. They tend to be the more strong and silent types. Kvasir's tend to find those who are more knowledge bound, seeking out those who have a love for learning and cannot seem to stop. Each god has their preference, both major and minor gods, and it is almost always people like them who find their relics."

"There have also been a few cases of relics being handed down as family heirlooms; sometimes the family already had a relic bearer who gave the relic to their descendants. Other times they were unaware of what they had, simply handing down some ancient trinket. Somewhere farther down the line there tends to be a member of the family who can wield the relic and its powers. I know of one case where a relic was passed from mother to son, granting both of them its powers, but such a thing is exceptionally rare."

"What scholars cannot seem to agree on is whether it is the relic or the god who chooses the wielder. Undoubtedly the gods have some knowledge of our presence, since they tend to impart small pieces of wisdom to us – some of them seem to just like to chat – but no one knows whether they have a hand in our choosing or leave that to their artifacts. However, if Thor said that Elena had been picked, I would certainly think they have some hand in the matter."

"Have there been any famous relic bearers in history?" Elena asked.

George chuckled. "My dear, there have been many. The most easily recognized would be Hitler. Even mortal history makes mention of his fascination with the Norse."

"What?" Liam was dumbfounded. "Hitler had a relic? What god would choose him?"

"He may even have had several. Scholars are still debating what relic he had, or who it was from. The most common theory is Loki, whispering dark thoughts into Hitler's dreams until insanity overtook him. Thor is another commonly suggested, for he loves battle and may have prompted Hitler to thoughts of war. However, it is agreed that he possessed at least one relic, and spent the rest of his life searching for more."

"As you have no doubt heard from your companions, the relic bearers swore an oath to not involve themselves in mortal politics – which, of course, made matters difficult upon the beginning of World War II. The council was divided, and in the end each acted as they saw fit, effectively leading to the dissolution of the council. There were many relic bearers who fought in the war, seeing it not as meddling in the affairs of the world; rather, they saw it as enacting their promise to bring down those who would use their relics for evil."

Liam shook his head. "Why would the gods allow something like that to happen?"

George shrugged. "You must remember that to the gods, our lives are short. Wars have always happened amongst men, and perhaps always will. How much notice they take of us and our warmongering is unknown. Think also on the fact that what to us are powerful objects are to them for the most part merely discarded knickknacks. Most relics are simply shards of one of the gods' tools – you two seem to be the exception rather than the rule. It is quite possible that whatever god had left behind Hitler's relic did not know how it was being used; or, if it was a relic of Loki, that he knew and was influencing Hitler to some degree. That is the theory I support."

They were silent for a moment before George shook his head. "But enough of such serious talk – you have only just awakened, and it is high time for breakfast. I believe Tom has some things laid out in the kitchen, if you'd care to follow me."

They nodded, Kieth with enthusiasm. Liam paused at the door as they headed after George, reaching out a hand to stop Elena. "Hold on a minute," he said with a frown. "Thor wants to say something."

She looked at him quizzically while he cocked his head to the side, listening. After a moment he nodded. "He says he's sorry that you had to experience his conversation with Loki. He didn't know you'd be able to see or feel any of that, and he is very sorry for any pain he caused you."

Elena shook her head. "Please, it's alright. It needed to be done – besides, I think I would've felt the pain anyway."

Liam grimaced. "Thor suggests using sleeping pills before bed; he says it can muddle the mind during sleep and make it harder for the gods to communicate. You shouldn't get quite so much feedback from Loki then."

"But I'm the only one inside his head. We need to have some idea of what's going on; a little pain is well worth being forewarned."

Liam paused before giving a short laugh. "He says that he bows before your bravery and that there is a spot in Valhalla awaiting you for your courage. I rather agree with him – and I'm sorry as well for my part in what happened."

Elena blushed. "Thank you – both of you – for the apology as well. And Liam, I'm sorry if I worried you when I woke up. It was just such a shock-"

"Don't, please. I'm just glad you're alright." He smiled at her. "It can't be easy being inside his head."

"It's…twisted, definitely, but fascinating. After having read so much about him, to finally see some of how his mind works…he's completely insane, but he doesn't think so. And his ego is astounding."

Strange. I would have thought he would guard his mind better.

Liam began to pass on Thor's thoughts, but Solveig leaned around the corner and interrupted him. "Are the two of you coming?" she asked impatiently.

"Sorry!" they said in unison, both jumping at her sudden appearance. They followed her sheepishly into the kitchen, trading a grin as they did so.

The kitchen was well lit, both by a window overlooking the sink and by a skylight; Liam assumed the room was an offshoot of the house, since otherwise the second story would have covered it. The floor was a cream tile, the cupboards made of a light wood. An oven and a dishwasher stood at opposite ends of the room, separated by a tall wooden counter lined with drawers and topped by a marble slab.

Atop the slab stood platters bearing toast, muffins, pancakes, eggs, and bacon, all cooling. Next to a sink on the other side of the counter stood a stove, and on one of its burners was a pot of steaming tea. Plates, mugs, and silverware had all been set out. Kieth was already serving himself.

"Will Tom be joining us?" Liam asked.

George shook his head. "Tom's a rather shy chap, and he normally takes his breakfast a bit sooner than this. Early riser and all that." He winked at them. "Not that you rose all that early – it's already almost noon. Even I've already eaten."

He held up a hand as they all started to speak at once. "Please, don't. I'm only teasing – you have all had a rather trying week. Enjoy your food; I'm going to head to the study. Please take your time, but when you're done, meet me there."

He wheeled out, leaving the four alone. Kieth was the first to shrug, digging into his plate. He was closely followed by Solveig, and Liam and Elena eyed the two in surprise. Kieth's plate bore a stack of five pancakes, two heaping ladles of eggs, and eight pieces of bacon; they rather suspected that the only reason he didn't have more was because he had run out of room. Solveig wasn't far behind him.

Fighting laughter, Liam said a silent prayer before beginning his own meal, Elena doing the same. They ate in silence, and despite the enormous amount of food he had taken, Kieth was the first to finish. "I'm going to see if George needs anything," he said after a few minutes of waiting. He set his dishes in the sink and left with a wave, Solveig following him soon after.

Elena and Liam finished more slowly, and afterwards Elena grabbed a cloth and began to wash the dishes. Liam found a towel and dried them as she handed them over. Both were quiet, unsure of what to say. Liam thought that he heard Thor snickering in the depths of his mind.

Finished, they headed to the study. There they found Kieth helping George to move books around. The room had been cleared slightly since the night before, but with five people it was still crowded. They huddled around the table or leaned against shelves, afraid to move for fear of knocking over a stack of books.

George ran a critical eye over the books spread over his desk. "Now then, here we are," he said after a moment. "The Ragnarök – the Doom of the Gods." He pointed to one volume that lay open before him, its pages yellowed and wrinkled with age. Upon one page were thick lines of a runic text that Liam vaguely recognized from Kieth's note. Upon the other stood a magnificently painted portrait of a burning tree surrounded by darkness.

"The basics I assume you know, but this volume goes over them. The day of the doom will come upon us, and Sköll and Hati shall swallow Sun and Moon, respectively. After this the stars themselves will fall, etcetera, etcetera..." George's finger moved down the page of text, and Liam realized with shock that the older man was translating the text for them on the fly.

"Let me see...then the earth shall shake until Fenrir's bonds are broken – Fenrir, of course, being the great wolf-" He looked expectantly at Liam.

"Right, Loki's son who swallowed Týr's hand and was imprisoned in Hel." George nodded and returned to his text as the others looked at Liam in surprise. He shrugged. "I did some reading last night."

George continued his deciphering. "'Then the World Serpent too shall come upon us, breaking free from his circle of the seas at last.' By this time Loki will have somehow been set free and will attack the gods on a ship from Hel. 'Then the sky itself shall crack open and the fire giants of Muspellheim shall come through, bringing war to the gates of the gods.'"

He looked up at them, his face grave. "A great battle will take place upon the plains of Vigrith, and the gods shall call upon all of their allies – but in the end it will be in vain. Though they will defeat many of their foes, most will die in the process...and Surtr, leader of the fire Jötun, will set Yggdrasill aflame."

"After this what few gods are left shall rise up into a new pantheon, and the two humans who survive shall repopulate the earth – but I rather think that isn't of too much concern to us, since that would mean we had failed." He shrugged and gestured to the other books spread out over his desk. "These other volumes contain pretty much the same information, with only trivial differences."

George peered at them over the top of his spectacles. "What remains to be seen now is what use this information is to us. As we have discussed, Odin must have wanted you to know all of this for a reason. However, last night he was silent to me, and I cannot see what he would have you do. These legends have been around for centuries, and I'm not sure how the All-father thinks they can aid us."

"Perhaps it won't make sense until we've heard all of what Odin wanted you to tell us," Elena said after a moment. "I only know a little about the Norns besides the basics – what can you tell us about them?"

"Yeah," Liam added. "I read about them last night, but there wasn't much information on them."

George sighed, closing his book and leaning back more comfortably into his chair. "That is because very little is known about the Norns. They are three sisters – Urd, Verdandi, and Skuld – that guard one of the wells beneath the roots of Yggdrasill. There they tend to the tree and keep it from rotting. They are also tasked with the spinning of the thread upon which hangs the life of everyone and everything – the fate of the universe, quite literally in their hands."

"These facts are all that is known for certain. As to the rest, there is only speculation based off of some myths, but not all, and sometimes the clues are openly contradicted in other myths. They are said to be able to read the future; this is why they can spin the thread. Their names offer us another set of clues, for Urd means both Fate and Past, Verdandi, Present, and Skuld, That-Which-Is-To-Be – or the Future."

"Where did they come from?" Solveig asked, curious.

"It is said that they once were giants, maidens from Jötunheimr. Of course, some others say that they are of the Valkyr. No one quite knows where they come from, though there are many theories, but it is generally agreed upon that Asgard knew nothing of time until their coming. The only way to reach their current dwelling is by using the Bifrost, the great Rainbow Bridge of the gods."

"It is also said – again, only in some legends – that the Norns will offer advice to any humans they deem worthy, either by visiting them in dreams or by a mortal somehow stumbling across their location. The advice is always given in the form of a riddle, and the proper questions must be asked for them to give it."

"Could that be the answer, then?" Kieth asked. "Find the Norns and ask them what we're supposed to do?"

George shook his head. "I very much doubt it. They have been sought after by many, and found by few. I wouldn't even know where to begin looking for them, and I suspect it would be their choice as to whether or not you found them."

Oh, finding them is easy enough. You just need to follow the rainbow.
Liam blinked. "Thor says to follow the rainbow."
George raised one eyebrow. "I beg your pardon?"

You said yourself, their realm lies over the Bifrost. All you have to do is cross the rainbow, and you'll find them.

The others looked on in surprise, Kieth struggling against laughter as Liam passed on Thor's words.

"My good sir, the sun is almost down and the sky is remarkably clear today. How would I go about finding a rainbow?" George asked.

Liam got the distinct mental image of a shrug. *You could always ask.*

Elena laughed. "Worth a try, I suppose. Where is the nearest rainbow, if you please?"

No, no, not me! Call for the Bifrost.

"I thought only the gods could use the Bifrost," Liam replied.

Don't your legends say that the fire Jötun will cross it come the Ragnarök, shattering the bridge? Besides, three of you have gods within you. But I'd hurry, if I were you – its destruction is fast approaching.

Liam finished relaying Thor's words, and George frowned. "Alright," he said after a moment. "Bifrost, we need to see the Norns."

For a moment nothing happened, and Liam was half convinced that Thor was pulling a prank. Soon, however, a faint shimmering light began to appear. They all crowded around the window, searching for the rainbow as the sparks grew ever brighter. Colored lights began to reflect around the room, greens, blues, and pinks bouncing off of the walls, and after a moment Thor laughed.

You're looking the wrong way, genius! You called for the bridge – it's not going to make you walk to it.

Liam whirled around, his jaw dropping in shock. Before him stood a shimmering gate, composed of all the colors of the rainbow. The doors swung open as he watched, a bridge beyond them extending up and into the distance until it faded from view, the ceiling no longer visible where it touched. At his gasp the others followed his lead and turned, their reactions similar.

Unfortunately, the terrain around the Norns is rough, Thor said after a moment of snickering at Liam's shock. *Your chair may have difficulties, old one.*

Liam relayed this to George, who nodded, unsurprised. "Supposedly a maze awaits beyond," he said. "I'd only slow you all down. Go on – I'll keep an eye on things here. Just make sure you can describe *everything* to me when you get back."

"We're honestly gonna ride that thing?" Kieth asked, looking at the bridge with trepidation.

Solveig shook her head. "I must admit, I have some qualms with this plan as well. But as it seems to be our only option…" She trailed off, still staring at the bridge.

It was Elena who stepped forward first. "If the gods ride across it with chariots, I think we'll be okay. Besides, you can *fly*," she glowered at Solveig, "So quit griping! If we do fall, I'll just use my shoes."

She set foot on the bridge gingerly, taking a slow step forward. The rainbow held, seemingly solid, and she relaxed as she looked back at them. "Come on, then! Oh, but be careful, Liam – as I recall, Thor couldn't use the bridge because his lightning would upset the 'delicate balance'."

Liam took a distinct pleasure in feeling Thor's discomfort. *I don't need any bridge,* he grumbled, and Liam laughed. "I just won't use my hammer, then. Thanks for the warning."

She shook her head, Thor adding, *It's not that simple. Mjolnir bears the weight of the storms – even its mere presence could disrupt the Bifrost.*

Liam grimaced. "What if I shifted it?"

The others watched his one sided conversation curiously as the god replied, *Not good enough. Shifting it merely changes its appearance – its abilities remain the same. You'll have to leave it here or stay behind, I'm afraid.*

"Well, I'm not staying." He turned to George, holding out his hammer. "May I leave this with you?"

George's eyes widened, his shock at being asked to guard such a powerful relic obvious. "I- I would be honored," he forced out. "If Thor does not mind?"

Can't think of anyone better, old one. Take care of it.

Liam gingerly set the hammer on the floor, remembering how heavy Elena had found it, as he relayed Thor's message. Then he too mounted the bridge, walking tentatively at first but gaining confidence as his footing held. Kieth and Solveig followed, and they turned to wave goodbye to George only to find the study gone, replaced by deep blue skies, stars, and barely visible clouds far below them. The rainbow beneath their feet lit their path in a manner reminiscent of tie-dye, casting neon colors upon their surroundings. It carried on into the distance, and seeing no other choice, the group continued forward.

They walked for a short time, learning quickly to not look at the sky while they did so. The constellations seemed to shift with every step that they took. "How fast are we moving?" Elena asked. Kieth, curious, braved a step while looking off to one side. The stars raced by, and it was only by dint of Solveig catching his elbow that he did not fall.

He murmured a thanks to her as she released his arm, the others breathing sighs of relief at her quick reflexes. Her eyes were wide at his close call, but she shook her head, calming herself. "I know not what distance we travel – only that the Bifrost allows travel of paths that would otherwise take a lifetime."

Several steps later the bridge began to curve downward, and all sighed in relief. Though beautiful, the scenery was eerie, with no noise save for that of their breathing and a faint swishing sound that brought to mind the boughs of a tree.

A few steps more and they reached the bottom of the bridge, emerging unexpectedly from another gate. This one opened onto surroundings as strange as those they had traveled through.

They stood beneath a high ceiling of what appeared to be earth, though it was darker than normal and lit by starlight that seemed to shine through the dirt itself. To either side of them and behind were rough stone walls of a natural formation, though they saw that an outline of a gate had been carved with runic symbols.

Elena seemed inclined to stay and decipher the runes, but the others pulled her with them towards what lay before the gate. It was a huge entryway to a long corridor, the walls here appearing to be a worked stone, though it still looked quite natural. To either side of the entry were more engraved runes, and these Solveig translated for the group.

" 'fore you may ask your questions, you must pass this test,
 For you to question the Norns, their halls you must best.' "

"Seems straightforward enough," Liam said. "A maze, like the legends say. How bad can it be?"

Elena hissed in dismay. "Don't say that! Great, now it's going to be super tough."

They looked at her and she blushed. "First rule of roleplaying – never challenge the creativity of the dungeon master."

Kieth and Liam laughed, though Solveig shook her head. "Let us hope it *is* simple."

They entered with Liam leading and Solveig guarding the rear, her sword drawn. Scarcely had they all passed through the entrance when a grinding noise filled the air. They whirled about in time to see a large boulder fall over the entrance, sealing them in. The four exchanged looks before Elena took a deep breath. "I guess we're going forward, then."

A thought struck Liam as they began to move through its walls. "Do you know the maze, Thor?"

Yes, but I'll not tell you how to navigate it. This is a test of your character, and must be completed by the four of you.

"Alright, then. Let's try left hand rule." The others nodded in agreement.

They headed down the hall until they came to their first turn. As Liam began to swing left, Thor uttered a curse. *Not that way!*

I thought you weren't helping! Liam thought.

Well, I didn't think that you would be foolish enough to go widdershins! Don't you know it's bad luck?

Liam jumped as Elena touched his shoulder. "Are you alright?"

He nodded. "Sorry, yeah. Thor says to not go that way – it's something called widdershins and therefore bad luck?"

58

Her eyes widened. "Of course, how stupid of me! We should head sunward."

Kieth shook his head. "Sorry, what exactly are widdershins and sunward?" He winked at Liam as the cop looked at him in gratitude, glad to not be the only one who didn't understand.

"Counterclockwise and clockwise, respectively. Or left and right," Solveig offered. "I had forgotten how much of a part they played in the old days. Thank you, Thor," she said with a slight bow to Liam.

They headed right, Solveig now leading while Liam followed behind. He shook his head. *Yes, thank you,* he agreed after a moment.

My pleasure. But really, the rest of the test is yours.

As they progressed through the maze, their surroundings changed. It soon became obvious that they were traveling in the right direction simply by the architecture. While the start of the maze had been primitive at best, they were now traveling into more refined and modern areas. The further on they traveled, the more futuristic the walls became, changing from stone to marble to brick to metal, the changes somehow blending seamlessly.

Traveling sunward seemed to work for the most part, with them running into only one or two dead ends. Each time they were forced to backtrack only a short distance before once again finding the correct path.

When they rounded one last corner the end of the maze loomed before them. The group was unsure of how long they had traveled for, but all were glad at the thought of rest. *Well done!* Thor said as they passed through the exit. *But I think they made it easy for you.*

Liam didn't reply, too busy staring at their surroundings. Before them stood what appeared to be a huge, long tree root, hanging down into a large well. Looking up, Liam shook his head in amazement. The root trailed on and on into the sky, growing thicker and knobbier as it rose until it finally reached the base of what he assumed to be the trunk. Unfamiliar stars shone around the darkness of the wood and Liam blinked, returning his gaze to the ground hastily as a wave of vertigo swept over him.

They walked forward to consider the well, looking within it. It was huge, easily the size of a small lake, a comparison made more vivid by the fact that two swans swam within it. The water glowed with a faint white light, and sparkling currents seemed to rise from it into the air surrounding them.

"A strange place," Kieth said after a moment. The others nodded their agreement, eyes wide as they looked around.

A sudden voice from behind made them turn, and Elena gasped at what they saw. "Well done, heroes – you have bested our test."

In front of them loomed the dark entrance to a cave, from within which emanated a faint clacking noise. In front of the entrance stood a figure, obviously female but clothed in a shroud of gray. No skin showed upon her and her hood was raised, the deep cowl throwing shadow over her face until nothing could be seen. She raised one hand in greeting, the sleeves of her robe trailing over the ground as she did so.

Liam smiled at the woman, walking forward and taking her gloved hand. He bowed over it and planted a kiss on the air above her knuckles before straightening. A look of confusion suddenly came over his face and he shook his head, frowning. "Sorry. I'm…not entirely sure why I did that."

She laughed. "But I am. Hello, Thor."

Hello, Skuld.

"It's been too long. I see you're converting the mortal – Liam, is it?"

He nodded, disconcerted by her hood. Though her voice sounded young, he was unable to see her face. Even standing so close to her, the inside of the cowl appeared a fathomless hole.

He's alright, I suppose. Though I think I could have done better.

She laughed again, a light and airy sound, and Liam was suddenly struck by the realization that she could hear Thor. "What…can you read my mind?"

She is one of the Wyrd, Liam. She sees all, hears all, and knows all. She always has and she always will. She is eternal and ageless, a timeless beauty-

She cut in, her voice amused. "I see you still have your penchant for flattery – but you know it will get you nowhere."

Elena stepped forward. "Forgive me, ma'am, but we have come here on a matter of some urgency-"

"Ah, Elena! And Loki – yes, I can see you, skulking in the depths. You've done well, my dear, to resist his whispers."

She blanched. "I…thank you. Please, time is short-"

"Oh, hardly. My sisters and I know better than any just how long time can be. But you are right to worry – the flow of time is different here than it is in your realm. Ask then what you would of me."

They hesitated, and Solveig was the first to speak. "Are your sisters here, my lady?"

Skuld shook her head. "They are otherwise occupied. Of late our skills have been much needed – only one of us may pause from our work, and then only for a short time. We deemed that I would be best suited to answer your questions."

The group exchanged glances. "Alright," Liam said. "Judging from that, I'd assume you know the circumstances that led us here."

She nodded to him. "I know how and why you have come, and what you would know, but the proper questions must still be asked. There is a ritual to all of this, one that must be observed."

"What is the proper question?" Elena asked hopefully.

Skuld laughed. "I'm afraid it's not that simple, my dear. You must decide that for yourself. Only then are my sisters and I free to aid you, in our own particular way."

"How do we stop the Ragnarök?" Kieth asked.

She shook her head. "The Ragnarök cannot be stopped. It is inevitable, something that has been foretold since the dawn of time. We wove its coming long ago."

"Then what is the point of all this?" Solveig asked angrily. "Why go to all of this trouble if it cannot be avoided?"

Skuld turned to her, and though her eyes were not visible Solveig could nonetheless feel the piercing gaze of the Norn. "I said only that it could not be stopped. There is always hope, never forget that – just as there is always a purpose to everything Odin does."

Solveig began to speak again, but Elena stopped her with a light touch. "What would Odin have us do?" she asked.

Skuld's voice was pleased as she answered. "He would have you delay the inevitable."

"And how do we do that?" Liam asked.

Two pale shining lights began to glow where her eyes would be within the confines of the hood as Skuld threw back her head. Her voice grew deeper as she spoke and the sky around them darkened, casting shadows upon the pond and the two swans that swam within it.

> *"The wolves move fast, their chase begun*
> *They seek to swallow Moon and Sun*
> *The stars will fall, the earth shall shake*
> *The tree upon the wheel of fate*
> *The fire seeks to devour the gods*
> *Mere mortal men must best the odds*
> *They stand alone and tip the scale*
> *Are any left to tell the tale?*
> *While Æsir fight upon Asgard*
> *Four heroes stand the Earth's last guard*
> *Aid may come in the moment last*
> *Should they win, the danger shall pass.*
> *But should they fail, the Tree shall burn*
> *The Heaven's patterns cease to turn*
> *Nothing shall stand before the Flame*
> *For all in its path it shall maim."*

Slowly her head fell back, the light within fading. The ground remained shadowed as the four stared at her. Skuld took a moment to catch her breath before speaking, her voice returned to normal.

"That is all the aid I can offer, I'm afraid. And now I must return to my sisters; we seek to keep the string of the universe tied together. But take heart, dear ones, for the light of mortals has always shined brightest in the dark." She curtsied to them and they returned the courtesy, still mulling over what they had heard as she vanished.

"I am not sure how much good this did us," Solveig muttered after a moment. "She told us no more than what we already knew."

Kieth shook his head. "Not true. Now we know that we alone must stand against whatever forces attack Earth."

Solveig nodded. "Exactly! We already knew that the gods would be in their own battle, and that we would stand alone."

Liam frowned. "She said that we would tip the scale. That doesn't necessarily mean to the winning side."

They looked at him, Elena nodding her agreement. "I caught that as well – but at least now we know that there *is* hope."

Solveig grimaced. "Only to 'delay the inevitable'. Ragnarök will still happen, one way or another."

"Not while I can help it," Liam murmured. "She said that the 'fire seeks to devour the gods'; does that mean we won't be facing the fire giants? And what did she mean by 'aid may come in the moment last'?"

All mused for a moment. "Well, we haven't seen any fire giants yet, and all the tales I've read have had them only ever attacking Asgard," Elena offered. "As to the last, it pretty much speaks for itself. We might have help at the last minute, or we might not. I'm more interested in who the help will be coming from."

Liam nodded. "Thor, did you catch all of that? What are your thoughts?"

That Skuld was in more of a sharing mood than normal. The first part of the prophecy we already know – and you're correct in saying that the fire Jötun will only strike Asgard. Ours is the only realm connected to them, and we stand as the last line of defense between them and the other realms. Should we fall, you'll have to deal with them – and if that's the case, all is lost.

He paused for a moment as Liam relayed this to the others, continuing, *You will fight, though I know not what. Perhaps only the armies of the other Jötun, but others might stand with them. I likewise do not know where your aid will come from, though I doubt it will be from the Æsir. Maybe the other relic bearers? I do not believe that you will stand alone – surely your mortal armies will aid in the battle if it is so grave– but it is clear that you and you alone are the key to our salvation.*

"So no pressure, right?" Elena said weakly after Liam finished speaking for the god.

The god laughed within Liam's head. *I like her. Though no warrior, she shows bravery in the face of battle.*

I like her too, Liam replied silently. Out loud he added, "We should go. She said time travels differently here, and that last part of the prophecy was pretty ominous…"

The others nodded. "I wonder what we will find upon our return," Solveig murmured, turning back to the maze. She gasped and the others turned as well, hands falling instinctively to their weapons.

Their eyes widened in shock as they stared. Behind them stood the gateway through which the Bifrost had deposited them, the maze having completely disappeared. Thor chuckled inside Liam's head. *I wondered how you would react.*

You knew this would happen? Liam replied.

Of course. The test had already been passed – why make you walk through it again when the fate of the universe is in danger? All of the Æsir have solved the maze, and none of us have been made to walk it again.

Liam shook his head as Thor laughed at him. He found the others watching him curiously and explained, "Thor says we only have to go through the maze once. He was waiting to see our reactions." Elena laughed, shaking her head at the god's actions.

"Bifrost, we need you," Solveig called out. "Return us to Midgard, please."

With a shimmer the Bifrost lit the gate once more, ready to take them home.

Odinsday

I dreamt of war for the first time since I was a young man – not the glory filled dreams of my youth, but of the horrors that I now know to be the reality of battle. It was so realistic, so graphic, that when I awoke I rushed to the window – only to see the same images of death and destruction. It was only then that I truly awakened.

George was waiting for them when they returned through the gate, and he seemed to have aged a year in the short time they'd been gone. His face was haggard as he spoke. "Come and see," he said grimly as they crowded once more into the study. He wheeled over to a window and they followed as the light of the Bifrost disappeared.

The sky had grown dark. Liam glanced at the grandfather clock that was crammed between bookshelves, remembering Skuld's words of how time passed more slowly in her domain, but the time took him by surprise. "It's mid-afternoon," he murmured, looking once more into the darkness.

There was a red tint to the sky that looked almost like a crack, but no other visible light could be seen. George nodded gravely. "You were gone for almost a day." He held up a hand, silencing their remarks. "This happened just a few hours ago. It's all over the news – it's not just our area. The sun and moon have disappeared."

Elena shook her head. " 'The wolves move fast, their chase begun'," she murmured.

" 'They seek to swallow Moon and Sun'," Liam finished. "We need to talk," he said to George.

The man nodded and settled into his chair, gesturing for the others to make themselves comfortable. Liam paused to grab Mjolnir from where it still rested on the floor before leaning against one of the bookshelves. "The television is on the fritz," George said as Elena glanced at the static filled box. "If I had to guess, I'd say the satellites are messed up. Radio still works sometimes, though – that's where I got my news. Now, what happened?"

They related their tale to him. George mused over the poem for a few minutes but reached no new conclusions, save for the fact that he would not stand with them. " 'Four heroes must stand'…that seems pretty clear. I'd probably just slow you down anyway."

Elena shook her head. "You're not going to be standing with us – you'll be sitting." She gestured to his chair and all laughed, though he still shook his head.

George's eyes lit up like a boy's on Christmas as they described Skuld to him, and he chuckled. "I wish I'd met her," he said. "She sounds just like everything I've ever read."

There was silence for a few minutes after they had finished. It was Solveig who broke it. "If we are to combat the Ragnarök, where will we do so?" she asked. "We have been given no further instructions as to where to go, though I suppose there is a certain irony in the end of the world taking place in New York, as it seems to in so many movies."

"All the myths I've read have it taking place in the fields of Vígríðr," Elena said, George nodding his agreement. "Although..." she hesitated. "Truth be told, I've never heard if the fields are located in Asgard or in Midgard."

"Well, the poem said we stood Earth's guard, so I'd guess here," Kieth mused. "But then the gods would be here as well, and we'd be aided."

George gasped and held up a hand for them to wait, flipping through several pages of one of his ever-present books. "Ah, I thought as much. The dimensions of the field are given – a hundred and twenty leagues in every direction. Why not assume that means vertically as well as horizontally? Perhaps the fields of Vígríðr are located in *both* Asgard and Midgard, one simply occupying the space directly above or below the other. The gods will fight upon one front, and we upon another."

"That's great, but where are the fields?" Liam asked.

George looked at him severely. "That's what I'm looking for, if you'll be patient. Perhaps you should ask Thor as well."

Thor? Liam asked.

What is it now, mortal? the god replied, a teasing note of longsuffering in his voice.

The fields of Vígríðr?

What of them?

Liam blinked. *Weren't you paying attention?*

The god laughed. *Believe it or not, I have better things to do with my time than to follow you around all day. We're slightly busy up here too. What is it you would know about the fields?*

Where are they located? Liam asked.

There was a pause. *Do you know, I'm actually not sure. It's been foretold for so long that everyone knows the name, but I've never heard the location mentioned. Does George not know?*

Liam shook his head. *He's looking.*

Tell him to ask my father.

The cop glanced up. "George, Thor says he doesn't know. He says you should ask Odin."

George grimaced, taking off his spectacles and rubbing his eyes. "Odin has been silent of late; I would think he would be busy with preparations. I've tried asking him."

Elena shook her head. "Perhaps there's only so much he can tell us. Odin's always been able to see the future, but he's only ever told even the other gods so much."

"Perhaps, but that is still of no use to us. I will ask again, but I do not expect an answer. For now, shoo – you have the run of the house. If I learn anything I'll let you know. And if Thor thinks of anything," he added with a glance at Liam, "Come and tell me."

They filed out quietly, returning to the living room. Kieth flopped onto the couch as Solveig began to pace in front of the fireplace. Elena sat on the edge of a chair while Liam merely stood, staring into the distance.

After several minutes of silence Elena stood. "I'm going to grab some food – do you guys want anything?"

"Mmm…food," Kieth purred. "I could stand some food."

That brought a laugh, easing the tension, and he grinned. Solveig chuckled. "As could I, I suppose."

"I'll help," Liam offered, and he and Elena headed to the kitchen. Tom was inside preparing a pot roast, and he glanced at them as they entered.

"Welcome back," he murmured shyly. "Give me a minute to put this on and I'll pull out the sandwich stuff."

They both thanked him, leaning against one wall. He nodded, quietly opening the oven and sliding the tray in. Closing it, he set a timer on the microwave before turning to the fridge. He dug around inside it for several moments, emerging with lettuce, cheese, meat, tomatoes, and various condiments.

Elena hurried to help him set it all on the counter as he directed Liam to a cupboard with bread. Pulling down a loaf, Liam grabbed a cutting board and a knife and began to slice.

"So what's your story?" Elena asked Tom as they assembled the sandwiches. "George told us that you're a relic bearer."

He nodded, not looking up. "I'm a retired Seeker, actually. George needed someone to look after him and I volunteered."

"What happened to him?" Liam asked, curious.

Tom shrugged. "Nothing yet, but I'm here to prevent anything from happening. With his movement being limited, we thought it was best to have someone watching over him – he has made some nasty enemies in his years."

He laughed at the looks on their faces, the duo obviously trying to decide what questions to ask first. "He hasn't told you much about his life, has he?" As they shook their heads, he continued. "George is a Vietnam vet. He was injured in the war, finding his relic shortly thereafter."

"What is his relic?" Elena asked.

"A discarded eyepatch from Odin himself, left over from the days when he wandered the earth freely. George wears it around his wrist. As I understand it, the patch was in a secret compartment of a drawer in a library they turned into a makeshift hospital. Anyway, George's injuries earned him an honorable discharge, and he returned to the books he'd loved growing up to explain what he had found."

"It was quite a few years before a Seeker discovered him – my mother, in fact. He hadn't used his powers much, and bearers of Odin's relics are always harder to find; their powers tend to be more subtle, just increasing knowledge rather than anything flashy. Though they do tend to have an affinity with birds…"

By this time the sandwiches lay forgotten, long since completed. "You said he'd made enemies. How?" Liam asked.

Tom shrugged. "Over his years with the Order George served as the library keeper. He researched all of the old manuscripts and learned quite a bit. I don't know how much you've heard of the Order, but one of their duties is to stop any relic users who choose to use their powers for evil. George was the researcher back at headquarters, supplying those who went out to fight with the information they needed to beat their enemies. I'd imagine quite a few want him gone; besides that, there are a few mythological creatures that would love to kill off anyone in the Order."

"George said he knew of one case where a relic passed from mother to son," Elena said slowly. "Was that you?"

He blinked. "Yes, it was. I'm surprised you'd think of it."

"What's your relic?" Liam asked.

"The sole of one of Hermod the Swift's sandals. I keep it in my own shoes."

Liam frowned for a moment, Elena giggling at his confusion. "He was one of Odin and Frigg's sons, known for his swiftness."

"Gotcha. And what does it let you do?" he asked Tom.

"Run really, really fast. Which is good for a Seeker, but not as cool as some relics. I don't get to use it much anymore," he replied.

Tom laughed as Kieth suddenly poked his head around the corner. "Oh, hey Tom. Aren't you guys done yet? We're starving in here. Too much longer and Solveig might fly into a rage."

She too leaned around the corner, glowering at the berserk. "I believe that would be you."

All laughed, Kieth eyeing the sandwiches as he did so. Elena turned to Tom with a smile. "Would you like to join us?"

He shook his head with a rueful grin. "Thanks for the offer, but I was up most of the night with George. I think I'll check in on him and then head to bed early."

He waved as he walked out. Liam called after him, "Thanks for talking!" When the cop turned back, Kieth was already halfway through his first sandwich.

Liam and Elena both said a quiet grace before grabbing their own, and Solveig waited until they had finished to ask what they'd been talking about. The duo related the tale, Solveig and Kieth's eyes widening as they described George's role in the order.

"You know," Liam said after a moment, "I've noticed an awful lot of similarities between Greek and Norse mythology. I mean, Hermod the Swift? Sounds an awful lot like Hermes to me. And Thor is a lot like Zeus-"

Please. I am far superior to that egotistical drama queen.

Liam jumped. "Wait, so you mean the Greek pantheon actually does exist too? And welcome back, by the way."

The others looked at him curiously as Thor replied, *Of course they do. You didn't think it was just us running around, did you?*

Liam related the comments of the god to the others. Elena frowned. "I always assumed the myths just spawned from the same location. I kind of figured you guys were the basis for all of them."

A distinct image of Thor shaking his head filled Liam's mind. *No, there are others out there. We try not to meddle too much in each other's affairs – it can be similar to your mortal politics but with more explosions.* They laughed as he continued, *Unfortunately, this is a matter for another time. I've things to attend to on my side – you lot be careful!*

They said farewell and Liam felt him withdraw, the sensation almost like a door being closed with just a crack left open.

"Well, that was interesting," Solveig said after a moment. She and Kieth both eyed the last sandwich hungrily. The lifkyr solved the problem by drawing her knife, chopping the sandwich in two. They split it evenly, Kieth nodding his thanks. "But I agree with Thor – it probably is a matter for another time."

"Like when the world isn't about to end?" Kieth asked in between bites.

"That might be a good time, yes," Solveig replied dryly. Liam and Elena chuckled, but there was a nervous edge to it as the group was reminded of what was to come.

Elena broke the tense silence. "Do you think we can stop it?" she asked.

Kieth mused for a moment, swallowing before he answered. "Skuld obviously thought there was hope. And if Odin can see the future, I doubt he'd arrange all of this just to have us fail."

"But he can see several possible futures – survival might only be one of them."

Liam shrugged. "Then we just have to make sure that one is the one that happens."

Elena shook her head. "Do you really think it's that simple?"

Solveig gazed at Elena curiously, then nodded. "I do. And I have to wonder why you think differently – you have been so positive throughout all of this."

The librarian blinked. "I – I don't know. I am being rather negative, aren't I?"

Kieth tapped her head. "Make sure you only listen to your own thoughts, alright?"

She nodded, looking down. "I'm sorry. I didn't even notice, but now that you mention it I'm seeing everything in a different light. He's very subtle."

"We'll help you out as best we can," Liam offered, patting her shoulder. She smiled up at him with gratitude.

"Thank you; I really appreciate it. I think it might be best if I tried to relax for now, maybe take a hot bath. I'd rather not sleep until I've cleared my head some."

They nodded. "Relaxing sounds good," Kieth agreed lazily as he licked his fingers clean of the few crumbs that clung to them. "And speaking of voices, I can hear the couch calling my name…"

Everyone laughed, enjoying the camaraderie for a moment longer before splitting ways. Solveig nodded towards where Gunnar grazed outside, remarking that he had probably missed her as she headed for him.

Elena emerged from the bath toweling her hair dry. She glanced into the study as she passed and found George asleep in his chair, a book still open on the desk before him. She smiled softly and closed the door to the study, thinking that he deserved whatever rest he could get.

Entering the living room she found Solveig polishing her sword. Elena shook her head as the lifkyr remained engrossed in her work, not even glancing up as Elena walked past. She smiled at Kieth, who was lounging on the couch with his eyes half closed, looking for all the world like a lazy cat. He nodded towards the front door as she glanced around for Liam, and she nodded her thanks as she headed out.

Kieth's gaze tracked Elena as she left the room before returning to Solveig, who sat before the fireplace cleaning her sword. He fought a laugh as he glanced at the clock, realizing that she'd been at it for almost an hour.

"If there are any stains left on it, I'm amazed," he murmured. She jumped, looking at him.

"I thought you were asleep," she confessed, but he shook his head.

"Just relaxing. But seriously, are you trying to blind your enemies with the sheen of the blade?"

She blushed. "Just trying to keep myself busy. I confess, I am envious of your calm."

Kieth shrugged. "Took a while to learn. How was Gunnar?"

"Ha! Quite indignant at my having left him for so long. He is a bit of a drama queen, but he is quite enjoying the grass outside."

The berserk cocked his head to one side. "Why don't you use contractions?"

Solveig frowned. "I beg your pardon?"

"Your speech. You almost never use contractions – it's always 'do not', 'I am', stuff like that."

She looked down, her cloth now running over the hilt. "When I was younger, I had quite the temper. I never really watched what I said, and I hurt quite a few people because of it. I had to learn to think my speech through before I said anything. To be honest, I have not really thought about it in a while."

"Ah – I'd wondered if it was a lifkyr thing." He grinned at her. "But I can understand what having a temper is like."

She glanced up, her eyes startled. "I apologize – I in no way meant to compare my problems to your-"

Kieth shook his head, laughing. "I'm not mad; I'm being serious. Although you are cute when you're flustered. And I can think of worse things than being compared to you."

She blushed, otherwise ignoring his comment. "All the same, at least I only had to change one aspect of my life. I cannot imagine what living as a berserk would be like…"

Solveig trailed off as Kieth nodded gravely. "I understand. But it's all I've ever known. If it helps, I can't imagine living as a lifkyr."

Her eyes sparkled. "Well, of course not. That's because only women are lifkyr."

Kieth laughed. "See? That wasn't so hard, now was it?"

She raised an eyebrow. "What was not hard?"

"You used a contraction. Didn't you notice?"

She blinked. "No, I – I did not."

"You've done that a couple of other times that I've heard too."

She shrugged. "I tend to not guard my speech as much when I am relaxed."

"So…does that mean you're relaxed around me?"

He chuckled as she blushed again, but Solveig met his gaze steadily. "Perhaps," she admitted. "But now that I know you're paying attention, I'll just have to add some in to freak you out."

Kieth blinked, one-upped. "Oh, that's just mean."

Liam leaned against the railing of the porch, staring up at the moonless sky. It was an eerie sight, the only light that of the steadily growing red crack. A sudden voice behind him made him jump.

"Strange, isn't it?" Elena asked, walking up and leaning next to him. "Especially this far from the city. It's so dark…"

He nodded, relaxing. "It almost seems as though we're the only ones in the world." He grimaced, realizing how much his words sounded like a lame pickup line. Elena appeared to not notice, simply nodding her agreement.

They stood in comfortable silence for a while, gazing up at the sky. Several minutes had passed before she spoke again. "Why are you a cop?"

He looked at her, puzzled. "I beg your pardon?"

She shook her head. "Sorry, rephrase – what's your story? Why do you do what you do?"

"Why do you ask?"

Elena shrugged. "Well, I've already heard the other's stories, and I get them to some degree. But you – you're more reserved, more quiet about your life."

Liam laughed. "Coming from you, that's pretty funny."

There was a short pause before Elena said, "I'd like to get to know you."

He hesitated, both of them fidgeting in the silence. Finally, Liam sighed. "The family that adopted me – their oldest son was a cop. He was kind of an inspiration to the youngest son and I, everything we ever dreamed of being. Then…he died when I was eleven, protecting some civilian on a drug bust that went wrong. After that, after all he had done, joining the force just seemed like the right thing to do. It felt like God was leading me there."

She looked at him intently, the strange horizon forgotten. "You were adopted?"

He snorted a laugh. "Not officially, but my real family life wasn't great. I spent most days at my best friend's house, and when his parents realized what my home situation was like they took me in. They raised me more than my own family did, taught me everything I needed to know about life."

"They sound like good people."

"Oh, they are. I still visit them during the holidays. People always laugh to see the gringo kid with the Hispanic family, but it's never mattered to us."

"And your friend, their son? What happened to him?"

"Jose joined the force as well. We room together in the city; still good friends, though we drive each other insane. He, uh," Liam shook his head, laughing at the memory. "He brought a dog home one time, even though our apartment then didn't allow pets. I was furious, but it turned out he was a stray who'd been abused. Jose always did have a soft spot for animals."

"We wound up moving so that we could keep him and found a nicer place with cheaper rent. The dog, Leeroy, he's been with us for three years now. We joke that he's our lucky charm." His smile faded after a moment as he looked up at the darkness. "I hope they're doing alright with all of this."

Elena put a hesitant hand on his shoulder. "I'm sure they're fine – Jose sounds pretty competent, and he's got a fierce hound to protect him."

Liam shook his head, chuckling, but squeezed her hand in thanks. "Not quite. The only way Leeroy could stop a thief would be by tackling him to the ground to lick his face. But I appreciate the thought."

Sudden laughter caught the duo's attention and both turned, glancing through the window to the living room. Kieth and Solveig were both caught in peals of laughter, and Liam and Elena exchanged looks.

"That *is* Solveig, right?" she asked.

Liam laughed. "Looks like her, but I'm not gonna rule out alien abduction. Seriously, though, I'm glad she's relaxing – she seemed pretty keyed up for battle."

Elena shivered slightly and Liam quickly shrugged out of his jacket, offering it to her. She took it with a smile. "Thank you – sorry, I was stupid and didn't think to grab one of my own."

He shook his head. "It's the middle of summer. Logic says it shouldn't be this cold."

She laughed. "True, but logic has little to do with mythology, as I'm sure you found out."

Liam quivered in mock horror. "Loki giving birth…brrrrr." He grinned as she laughed again, then turned to more serious matters. "Your turn – where are you from?"

She shook her head, quieting. "New York, but I've been in Arizona the past couple of years."

"You're joking! What city?"

She looked at him. "Tucson. Why do you ask?"

Liam cracked up. "I'm from Tucson too! Oh, that's just too much. What were you doing there?"

Elena shrugged, grinning. "School. I was going to the U of A." She hesitated for a moment before continuing. "The money wasn't for me, you know."

He looked at her in surprise. "What money?"

"From the house. I wasn't stealing to try and get me some extra cash – my dad got cancer and couldn't afford the chemo."

He nodded slowly. "I guessed as much from what you said to George… but why tell me?"

She shrugged again. "I didn't want you to think that I was just a selfish criminal."

He touched her hand gently. "I think I know you better than that."

Elena blushed, looking down. "You know, I was such an idiot. My father had plenty of friends like George that I could have asked for help, but it never even occurred to me. I just turned to my books, and they led me to burglary. It was my own fault that we couldn't afford the chemo, so I thought I had to fix it."

Liam frowned. "How was it your fault?"

"My father was thrilled that I wanted to follow in his footsteps and be a librarian. He said he'd pay my way into whatever college I chose – I was down at the University of Arizona because they have such a good Library Sciences program. I was about to finish off my Masters when we found out he had cancer. After that I learned that he'd used all of his savings to pay for my classes, and our insurance wouldn't cover the chemo."

"What did you do?"

She shook her head. "I dropped out and came home to be with him. I didn't have much spare cash, so I started looking for a job. When I couldn't find one, I decided that I'd do whatever I could to support him – even steal. I tried to pick a place that I knew could take a hit, and I was only going to take the books that the guy never read…it was my first job. And then I couldn't find that stupid ladder!"

Liam laughed. She looked up at him with a shy grin and he shook his head. "You turned criminal to support someone that you loved; I still don't agree with it, but I can't think of a better reason. Although I *am* going to tease you about this for a while - trying to steal a ladder."

She turned serious. "If we live through this, I'll look forward to it."

Liam hesitated, on the verge of saying more, but Solveig interrupted by leaning out the door. "Come quickly – George has found something."

They turned immediately, heading for the door, when a sudden white flash stopped Liam. He turned back, the others following him to see what was wrong. Wordlessly he stared at the sky, lit by the orange glow of the ever-widening crack – and gasped as another white streak shot past.

" 'The stars will fall'," Elena murmured as more and more began to shoot past. "We should hurry."

They headed indoors, disturbed by what they had seen. Kieth met them at the living room, straightening from where he leaned against a chair at the looks on their faces.

"What's wrong?" he asked worriedly. "Are you alright?"

"Everything okay?" George called as he wheeled into the room.

Solveig walked forward, grabbing Kieth by the elbow as she passed him and dragging him along behind her. He glanced down at her in surprise, the wiry lifkyr seeming small in comparison to the big man, but followed her without complaint. She led him to the window and pointed outside.

George pulled up next to them. "What are we looking for-" he began to ask, stopping in shock as he saw the streaks that shot across the horizon.

"Tell me you found something," Kieth murmured, his eyes fixed on the sky.

It took the old man a moment to respond. "Not as much as I would like," he finally managed, tearing his gaze from the spectacle outside. "But it may be something. Come with me."

They followed him away from the window, entering the study once more. The desk had been cleared of books, the tomes now stacked to all sides of it. They had been replaced by a variety of maps. George wheeled into his spot behind the desk, gesturing to the maps as he began to speak.

"Odin spoke to me while I dreamt; I don't remember all of what he said, but I know we spoke of islands. Remembering what you had said about not having received further instructions," he nodded to Solveig, "I narrowed down my search to islands in New York, looking for where the Ragnarök would take place."

"I don't understand," Liam interjected. "I thought the battle was supposed to take place on the plains of Vígríðr?"

"Yes, exactly!" George crowed triumphantly. "Which are supposed to be located on the fields of Óskópnir!"

The four blinked as he continued. "Knowing, thanks to Odin, that the fields were located upon an island, I began to search through my maps of New York. I've found several that might be the location based solely on their names."

"What are they?" Elena asked.

George shifted the maps sprawled across his desk, pointing to each in turn. "My first guess was Fire Island, since if the Ragnarök took place there the world would fall to fire – hence the name. However, the next island caught my eye as well; High Island, perhaps named after Odin's mortal alias. The third, which I judge least likely, is the Isle of Meadows; perhaps its name was mistranslated from fields or plains."

Elena frowned as the others pored over the maps. Something told her that none of these were the proper island. After a moment she leaned forward, pointing to another map that had been pushed aside to make room for the others. "What's this one?"

George looked at her. "This one...let me see." He pulled it out and glanced at it. The isles upon it were small, the writing difficult to see. "The Three Sisters Islands."

They all looked at each other in surprise. "I know of the place," Elena said slowly. "My father used to take me there when I was little."

"You don't think – the Norns?" Liam asked.

"But there's three islands," Solveig interjected. "Should we not be looking for only one?"

George gasped suddenly, pointing. "Kieth, the red book on that shelf there – bring it to me, will you?"

Kieth turned, searching momentarily for the book before finding it. He pulled it off of the shelf and passed it to George, who thanked him absentmindedly. The old man opened the book and began to flip through its pages.

Liam twitched as Thor made a sudden appearance. *What's new?*

George thinks he might have found Óskópnir's location. We're trying to finish narrowing it down now. How'd your stuff go? Liam replied silently.

Well enough, thank you, Thor began, but stopped whatever he was about to say as George grinned.

"Aha! I thought I recognized the name! The Three Sisters Islands have been a favorite amongst so called psychics for years, with many believing that anyone who goes to the islands can hear 'the voices of the spirits'. And look at this – 'Many years ago a Native American tribe offered sacrifices on the islands to one they called He-No – the Mighty Thunderer.' "

Oh, I remember them. They were a fun crowd, Thor said with a grin as the group looked at one another. *The realms always seemed closer together there; I think sometimes they* did *hear me.*

"Thor says he remembers them," Liam passed on. The five exchanged looks, and Solveig shook her head as she glanced at the map.

"The islands are not far from here," she said softly.

"Well done, my dear! Well done indeed!" George said to Elena, who blushed. "I would not have though of these if you hadn't said something."

She shook her head. "I don't know why I thought of it – the others just didn't seem quite right."

Kieth cocked his head to one side. "Why would the Ragnarök take place there, though? It doesn't seem too special. Not as big as some of the other islands."

Liam commented before George could. "Thor mentioned that the realms always seemed closer together there."

"Odd," the old scholar muttered. "I can't think why that would be."

"Perhaps it is just the way the world is made," Solveig suggested with a shrug. "We may never know. But I have been wondering – how have the Jötun been crossing into this realm?"

George shook his head. "As to that, I have only speculation. Perhaps as the Ragnarök nears the gateways between the realms weaken and become more easily traveled – who knows?"

"How long do we have?" Liam asked, looking over the map of the Islands. "Before the Ragnarök begins, I mean."

"Technically speaking it has already begun – but if you mean when the battle will begin, I would say not until the earthquakes start."

"Will we have time to get to the Islands if we don't leave until then?" Kieth asked.

"And will the quakes impact our travel time?" Solveig added. "Gunnar can avoid them, of course, but he can only carry two."

There was a slight cough from the doorway and all turned. Tom stood there apologetically, his flannel pajamas covered with a bathrobe and his feet clothed in fuzzy bunny slippers. "Sorry, I couldn't help overhearing – but I wanted to ask if you'd seen the sky. Are the stars supposed to be falling?"

They nodded. "Yes – well, no, but we knew it would happen," Elena tried to explain.

Tom paused, somewhat confused, but let the issue pass by. "Alright then. I figured you'd know what was going on, but I wanted to make sure. Did I hear that you might need to be somewhere quickly?"

George's face lit up. "Of course, why didn't I think of that? Yes, we think we've found the location of the Ragnarök. Come here and take a look."

Tom walked in shyly, peering at the map. "It's only about seventy miles from here. When do we need to leave?"

"We don't know," Liam said, shaking his head at Tom's question. The man seemed willing to leave at this moment, fuzzy slippers and all. "After the earthquakes start."

"Your shoes should be able to carry you just as swiftly, my dear," George said with a glance at Elena. "If your steed bears two of you, and Tom another, I think you should be able to get there."

Tom laughed. "It's been a while since I needed to move fast – this should be fun. Well, if I'm not needed tonight, is there anything else I can get you before I head back to bed?"

They shook their heads, thanking him and bidding him goodnight. He exited with a wave and George yawned, pulling off his glasses and tossing them onto the table. He rubbed his eyes, stretching, and the others started to feel the day catching up to them. "I think it's time for me to head to bed as well," the older man said after a moment. "I've the feeling we're all going to need our rest."

They nodded, but before he could leave Liam voiced a question that had been nagging at him. "I know everything seems to fit, but what do we do if this turns out the be the wrong island?"

Have a little faith, mortal; have a little faith! Thor said swiftly.

George's comment echoed Thor's sentiments. "Pray that it is the proper one – but do you have a cell phone?"

Liam shook his head, having lost his at some point after the Caves, but Elena nodded, pulling one out of her pocket. "I do."

"Good. We'll trade numbers – make sure you keep it on you. If I hear of something happening elsewhere, I'll call you."

They exchanged numbers, and Elena stuck her slip of paper into the pocket of Liam's jacket, still snug around her shoulders. Kieth broached another question to the old man. "Is it possible that the Order might aid us?"

George frowned and shook his head. "I'm afraid that over the years they've grown accustomed to members foretelling the Ragnarök – particularly old and senile ones like me. They've simply stopped listening to the rumors. If I were to go to them with what we know, they'd probably dismiss me as crazy; especially if I were to name the relics in your possession," he added with a glance to Liam and Elena.

Kieth shook his head and Solveig patted him on the arm. "It was worth a try," she murmured to him. He smiled at her.

George waited a moment more and then excused himself, saying a weary goodnight as he wheeled past. The group was quiet as they returned to the living room, settling into what were quickly becoming their normal spots.

After a bit Liam spoke again. "I know Loki's supposed to enter the final battle – how is he supposed to be freed?" he asked. "The books I read didn't say much."

Elena began to answer but then shook her head, the matter too close to her for her to be sure of anything. It was Solveig who answered him instead. "The earthquakes as Yggdrasill shakes were to free him from his prison, along with Fenrir."

Liam grimaced. Kieth, too, seemed disconcerted. "Then what was the point of imprisoning him in the first place?" the big man asked.

"I think they hoped they'd have more than a few days of peace," Elena responded quietly, looking at her hands. The other three looked at one another worriedly, Kieth quickly changing topics to try and ease Elena's mind.

"So I learned something today," he said with a grin. "Show them, Solveig."

Elena and Liam glanced at one another, surprised. "Show them what?" Solveig asked, her bearing innocent.

The big man laughed. "Oh, come on! You were doing so well earlier."

The lifkyr shrugged, chucking a pillow at Kieth before stretching out. "I am afraid that I do not know what you are talking about." She pulled a blanket over herself as Kieth gaped at her, Liam and Elena fighting laughter. "Good night, my friends. I'll see you in the morning."

"There! You heard her!" Kieth exclaimed.

Elena and Liam locked eyes and nodded, Solveig's smug smile telling them all they needed to know. "Heard what, Kieth?" Liam asked, feigning ignorance.

"Yeah, what's so odd?" Elena added.

"I – I…" He looked back and forth between the two of them, and Elena barely managed to keep a straight face. "Was there nothing strange about what she just said?"

The librarian shrugged, settling into her couch. "Nothing that I noticed. Goodnight!"

Liam bit back a laugh at the look on his friend's face. "Kieth," he said as he clapped the man's shoulder, "I think it might be best if you got some sleep."

Kieth groaned. "Fine, be that way. And don't think I can't hear you laughing!" he called to Solveig, who was furiously trying to muffle her giggles with a pillow. The man heaved a sigh, settling into his armchair. "Everyone's against me. I see how it is. Goodnight, you fiends."

Liam shook his head with mirth and flipped off the light.

Thorsday

I see the mugging taking place, the defenseless old woman struggling to beat off her attacker, and I race to help. The man strikes at me as I come close but I block, and as I do so I feel the rage begin to overtake me. I plead silently that it will not do so again, but to no avail; he yells insults at me as he advances with his knife raised, and my vision fills with red. When the blood finally clears from my gaze I hear screams from behind me – but the crimson will not leave my hands, dripping as I look upon the lifeless bodies of not one, but two victims...

I awake to a sound so incongruous that for a moment I wonder if I'm imagining it. It is a sound that has never before been heard in Asgard, but one that we have been trained to recognize since before the dawn of time. It is the call of Gullinkambi.

Sif sits up beside me, and even in my home of Bilskirnir so deep within Asgard, we know that we are not safe. Beneath us in the stables I can hear Toothgnasher and Toothgrinder bleating nervously.

My wife looks at me with fear in her eyes, her face grave. "Is it time?" she asks.

I nod silently, standing and pulling on my clothes. Instinctively I reach for Mjolnir, but it is not here – my thoughts turn to Liam, and I find him still asleep. Take care, little one, *I send his way.* Do not lose hope.

As ready as we can be, my wife and I leave our halls. Odin will have need of us.

In my prison I hear the sound that for so long I have longed for. Sigyn stares at me, her eyes wide, and I give thanks that this moment should come when I am lucid. The bowl is less than half full, a fact I am grateful of as her hands begin to shake.

"Surely it cannot be," she murmurs, staring in horror at the ceiling. She jumps as I begin to laugh.

"Oh, but it is. The time has come, wife!"

My laughter rises as the great rooster crows. Let Odin do what he will – now, I cannot be stopped.

Liam awoke to an odd sound, and for a moment he thought he was still dreaming – it was the sound of a rooster crowing. Blinking, he looked around blearily. The sky outside was lit with a smoky red, but without the sun he couldn't tell if it was dawn. Confused, Liam glanced at the others, who were also sitting up. He hadn't thought that George owned a rooster...

"Gullinkambi," Solveig whispered, shaking her head. "The day is upon us."

78

Elena flinched at the name as George came wheeling down the hall, looking disheveled in a flannel bathrobe. "Loki's thrilled – he thinks he can't be stopped now," she reported.

Liam frowned, listening for a moment. "Thor's talking to Odin. He says we shouldn't lose hope."

"Then is it time?" Kieth asked.

George grimaced. "I honestly don't know. I think it's safe to say that it's around dawn now – without the sun it's hard to tell, but that was when the great rooster was supposed to crow his warning. The call merely portends the day of the Ragnarök, however – not the hour. We may yet have some time-"

Two noises came suddenly, one atop the other, proving George wrong as the group cried out.

First came the horn – two short blasts followed by one long one that set their blood to racing. All reached for weapons on pure instinct, even Elena and George, the urge to fight so clear and overwhelming that it could not be denied.

Overlaying the last clarion call of the horn came a great *crack* as though a nearby tree had snapped in two. Moments later came a rumble of the earth that set the house shaking, knocking over those who had stood and toppling bookshelves. Glass shattered and wood split, furrows appearing in the walls – and, disconcertingly, the ceiling. With the quake came a heart rending fear and a soul-deep chill that struggled to overpower the battle lust the horn had awakened.

When the quake finally ended none could say how long it had lasted. Liam was too busy praising God for keeping the roof intact to even try. The group fought to compose themselves, the memory of the quake still making them shiver.

"What was that?" Liam forced out, his voice hoarse.

"The shaking of the World Tree itself," George replied, his own answer tight. He closed his eyes for a moment, struggling to calm his heart.

"The horn," Elena said, searching her memory. "That was Heimdallr calling us to battle, wasn't it?"

The thought of the call strengthened their defenses against the darkness, and all clung tightly to the memory. "Yes," George said, looking at her thankfully. "That was heard in all nine of the realms. The Æsir are calling their allies to battle.

There was a pattering of feet as a disheveled Tom came racing down the stairs. "Is everyone alright?" he called.

"We're good!" Liam replied. "Kieth, Solveig, you alright?"

Kieth coughed awkwardly, his face flushing red as he offered a hand to help Solveig up. A fallen bookshelf lay close to them, and Liam dimly recalled seeing Kieth take the blow of it to protect the lifkyr. "I think so," he rumbled back, though he flinched with the words.

Solveig's face was similarly flushed, but she was calm as she raised her hand to Kieth's face. The firelight revealed an already swelling bump from a fallen tome, and Kieth grimaced as she ran her fingers lightly over it.

He reached up and caught her hand. "Not the most heroic of battle scars," the big man murmured.

Her eyes met his evenly, the ghost of a smile flickering over her face as she squeezed his hand. "But gotten in defense of a maiden – surely that counts for something."

Kieth grinned sheepishly at her, laughing at Liam as the cop rolled his eyes. Liam righted George's fallen wheelchair and Tom helped the old scholar back to it. Liam had dived for George on pure reflex, knocking him aside just before a full bookshelf toppled into the space he had vacated, and Thor had let out a sigh of relief in his mind. Liam winced as George settled heavily into his chair, Elena hovering nearby. "Are you alright, sir?"

He waved them off. "I'll be fine – but I think it's safe to say that my adventuring days are over. Thank you for the rescue."

Elena, satisfied that there was nothing she could do to help George further, stepped over to Liam with a grin. "For the record, I think you were pretty heroic," she murmured, and he smiled at her.

It was Tom who coughed and brought them back on track. "Was that the earthquake we were waiting for? Because if not, I'd hate to think how bad that one will be."

George let out a shaky laugh. "As best as I understand it, that was it, Tom. We've little time if the horn has been sounded – you must go."

Liam shook his head stubbornly. "What about you, sir? If another quake comes, you won't be safe here."

George opened his mouth to protest but was cut off, to everyone's surprise, by Tom. "He's right, sir, and don't you argue about it. At least let me get you to safer ground while this lot has breakfast. There's cinnamon rolls cooling on the counter."

Tom flushed as the others stared at him but stayed resolute. "I couldn't sleep last night for wanting to help more, but I'm no warrior. I figured a decent breakfast was the least I could do."

"It's a great help, Tom, thank you," Kieth interjected as the butler paused for breath. "I, for one, am starving."

"Yes, but you're always starving," Solveig murmured. The others nodded their agreement as Kieth glowered at her, but she ignored it, striding towards George. She clapped him on the arm. "Fear not, old one – we shall hurry, and still make it in time."

George sighed in resignation as Tom began to roll him out of the room. "Fine, I see I'm overruled. But be careful, my friends! You'll be in my prayers."

Tom met them outside, where Elena was just finishing her last bite and Solveig was soothing Gunnar with the aid of an apple. "All set? Good," he said, rubbing his hands together. "He's as safe as I could make him, and chafing for the fuss," he added as Liam opened his mouth to ask after their host.

"Tom, you seem…changed," Solveig's tactful question was better than anything the others had come up with.

He let out a short, breathless laugh. "You mean not so shy? I figure, it's the end of the world, what do I have to lose? George is trying to contact the order, see if they can get you any backup," he added. "Once I drop you off, I'll try and do the same. How are we doing this?"

"I'm taking Gunnar, and *he* is coming with me," Solveig replied, glancing imperiously at Kieth.

"Who am I to decline such an invitation?" he answered with a grin. She rolled her eyes as he mounted up before vaulting onto the horse behind him.

"Well, since I can fly, I guess that leaves you with Tom," Elena said to Liam.

He nodded. "But stay close, alright? I don't think it's wise for us to split the party this late in the game."

She nodded, laughing, and Liam was struck suddenly by how beautiful she looked. "I knew there had to be a gamer in you somewhere! Stay safe, alright? All of you," she called back to Solveig and Kieth, who nodded as the lifkyr nudged Gunnar into motion.

Elena took off running after them, the sandals letting her move faster than Liam would have thought possible. Within seconds she was out of sight, leaving him alone in the clearing with Tom.

The butler extended his hand. "Are you ready for this?" he asked.

Liam grasped his arm, shaking his head. "No," he replied. "But lets do it anyway."

The storm clouds were roiling overhead as Elena landed. The others stood nearby, and Tom bid a hasty farewell before taking off to try and contact the council. A worried-looking Solveig whispered something in Gunnar's ear, then stood back to watch as he galloped away.

Thunder boomed, but there was no lightning. For the first time Liam felt Mjolnir grow heavy, as though the hammer longed to do a battle of its own amongst the clouds.

The ground was thick with snow and ice, the trees heavy with it, but for the first time in weeks it felt warm. Water dripped from the trees overhead as the snow began to melt, and somewhere out of sight the group could hear ice cracking.

Above them loomed the great fiery gap in the sky, so close to directly overhead that their necks strained as they looked at it. "It's grown," Elena murmured, the others nodding agreement.

Liam looked around. The place seemed deceptively calm for the supposed site of the Ragnarök – almost peaceful, really. "Are we early or something?" he asked.

Kieth groaned. "Maybe this is the wrong island."

Elena shook her head fiercely. "This is the right one; I'm sure of it!"

To everyone's surprise, Solveig agreed with her. "It has a feel to it – something old, and powerful. I believe we're in the right place."

"Call George," Kieth suggested. "See if he's heard anything on his end."

Elena nodded and grabbed the phone. "Oh, shoot! The battery's dead!"

A sudden thought struck Liam as the others groaned. "Let me see it, please." She looked at him quizzically before passing it to him.

Liam took hold of the phone, touching his finger to the charger plug. *Thor?* he asked quietly.

He felt the god roll his eyes. *The end of the world is here and you want me to charge your phone. Really?*

Nonetheless, a spark raced from Liam's finger to the end of the phone, and the cop fought to keep from jumping as the hairs on his arm stood on end. The screen immediately flashed white, a tone sounding as the phone turned on.

The others looked at him in surprise, and he shrugged. "Figured it was worth a shot."

You'll have to keep hold of it, Thor warned him, and Liam paused as he handed it to Elena.

"Thor says I have to keep holding it," he told her, and she nodded. Swiftly she dialed the number in her pocket, raising the phone to her cheek. Her hand settled over Liam's, and he might have blushed if he hadn't been trying so hard to keep from laughing as her hair rose from the static electricity.

"George!" she said after a moment. "We're here, and the crack looks like it's right on top of us, but nothing is happening!"

He said something Liam couldn't quite make out, and Elena nodded. "Alright, we'll wait. You're sure you haven't heard anything?" She paused for a moment, listening, and then nodded once more. "Okay. My phone's about dead, as a warning, so if I don't pick up don't worry – I'll try and call you back after a bit."

As she hung up, Liam dimly heard George asking how she would call if her phone was dead. He laughed, quieting when she handed him the phone. "Here – maybe it'll stay on if you keep hold of it."

There was no warning as the water around them exploded. The group reached for weapons as they turned to find the cause of the disturbance, but what they saw made them freeze in abject terror. Before them rose an enormous serpent, its scales a sickly green. Beneath the red light of the sky it was an image of horror, its mouth open as it hissed to the heights. Its fangs were long, its open mouth easily towering over the oaks, and there seemed no way that it could possibly fit into the river.

"Jörmungandr," Elena gasped. "But – he was supposed to fight Thor!"

I'm otherwise occupied! You'll have to keep him busy! The god shouted.

The others jumped, looking around, and it took Liam a moment to realize that they too had heard the god. Kieth muttered something about the closeness of the realms as the great serpent continued to rise from the waters.

As the berserk spoke the monster's head swung around, its beady yellow eyes locking on the four. "Yessss," it hissed. "I've hungered for sssso many yearsss – sssso kind of the godsss to arrange a ssssnack!"

Without warning it lunged forward, its huge jaws snapping shut on empty air as Elena became a blur, grabbing Liam and jumping for the trees. Solveig's tattoos enlarged into actual wings that glowed bright purple as she tackled Kieth, rising into the sky with him.

Trees splintered beneath the weight of the serpent as its head cracked rock where it struck. It shook its head, slithering upright once more and muttering what seemed to be curses in an ancient tongue. "Ssssuch sssmall morssselsss to be sssso troublesssome…"

Liam held tight to Elena as she dashed over to where Solveig was hovering with difficulty. The lifkyr and Kieth waved for them to keep going. "We'll handle it!" Kieth yelled as Solveig began to circle. "You go and make sure there's nothing on the other islands!"

Shrieking, the serpent struck at them, and the two groups once more dove to opposite sides. Though the creature was quick, it took the monster a while to recover from its pounces due to sheer body mass. Liam and Elena exchanged glances as Kieth yelled to get its attention before reluctantly turning to the next island.

"Father!" I run towards him as he steps off of the Bifrost. "Has Mimir spoken? Or is it truly the end?"

He shakes his head, his face grave. "He was silent. The great Doom is upon us."

I hesitate. "Father, Jörmungandr is on Earth. The mortals face him."

He looks at me, his surprise evident. "But you were to fight him-"

"I know. I wonder if by sending Mjolnir I have somehow altered the future. Can you see anything?"

Odin pauses for a moment, his eye unfocusing as he stares into the distance. After a moment he shakes his head, and I am struck by how much older he seems. "My vision is clouded – there are too many possibilities, too many variables."

I pause, considering my words before speaking – something that I believe I have picked up from the human. "I do not think that they can win alone."

He meets my gaze evenly. "Only you can make the choice, my son."

"But how? I cannot leave my family – but I cannot allow them to fight without aid."

He puts his hand on my shoulder, and something changes between us. No longer is one superior – for now, at least, we are equal. "Search your heart, and then follow it. You know what you must do, even if you cannot yet see it."

He glances behind me to where the others await his word. "I must go and prepare – we all must. But know this; whatever you choose, and whatever happens on this day, I am proud to call you my son."

I blink, my throat suddenly tight as he walks past me to meet with the rest of the Æsir.

Solveig waited until Jörmungandr struck once more, dodging to the side and lugging Kieth away. They landed heavily a short distance from the river, and the snake howled curses behind them as it struggled to rise and follow them. She panted, and Kieth could see that she wouldn't be able to carry him for long.

"Split up?" he asked quietly.

She shook her head. "Better to stay together, I think." They listened for a moment, hearing the splashing of the river as the serpent moved through it. She looked up at him, and though her face was calm her eyes showed fear. "It's been an honor knowing you."

Kieth smiled sadly. "Please. It's been a pleasure."

A sudden noise behind them startled them both into motion, diving to opposite sides. Jörmungandr swept his head down to where they had stood moments before, and both gave silent thanks for their inherited battle reflexes.

"Oi! Ugly!" Kieth called, fighting to keep his calm. The last thing he needed now was to lose his control. "Over here!"

It swung about to face him. "Who daresssss?" it hissed with rage.

Kieth bared his teeth at it. "That would be me," he growled, his hands extended as he shifted his weight. Out of the corner of his eye he saw Solveig draw her sword, the orange fire glinting off of the serpent's scales. He hoped that he could buy her some time – and that she would actually be able to damage the beast.

As Jörmungandr lunged towards him in fury Kieth took a few steps forward and leaped, drawing off of his size and momentum to fly over the striking teeth. He landed atop its snout and rolled, coming upright between its eyes. Gram flashed as Solveig swung for the neck, and Jörmungandr hissed in pain as the sword cut through several of its scales.

Kieth cursed as Jörmungandr rose. There was just too much mass to the serpent for the sword to do any good. He wavered and crouched on the indent between its eyes as its head rose above the trees, the serpent shaking its head from side to side in an effort to dislodge him. He held on to the scales grimly. Its eyes crossed, leaving him in the center of its gaze, and he fought to keep from shaking at the malevolence centered on him.

"Puny mortalsss," it called out, its voice vibrating beneath him. "Give up now and I sssshall make your deathssss quick!"

"Go to Hel!" Kieth replied, and Jörmungandr suddenly whipped its head to one side, sending him flying towards the ground. A purple and orange glow shot past and he heard Jörmungandr scream in pain as Gram made contact with a vulnerable spot – its eye.

Kieth closed his eyes as the ground rushed towards him, fighting a yell before he felt his arm caught in a vicelike grip. Solveig struggled to rise, her wings pumping furiously, but was only able to slow their descent. Both crashed to the ground, sending up a wave of dirt in either direction.

They coughed and struggled to stand, with Kieth the first to recover. He rose unsteadily, lending a hand to Solveig as she forced herself to her feet. Behind them they heard the serpent shrieking, spouting highly unlikely tales as to the origins of their ancestors.

Kieth braced Solveig as she shook. "I don't know how much more I can do," she panted, and he nodded understanding.

"You're pushing too far as is. I'd rather not have you taken up to Valhalla just before we beat this thing," he replied. She laughed shakily, and he grinned at her.

They began to run through the trees as the sounds of Jörmungandr's pursuit reached them. "Good thinking, going for the eyes," Kieth called as they ran. She nodded her thanks.

"I can't do any damage anywhere else," she said.

He blinked suddenly. "Wait a minute – your ancestor, Sigurðr – didn't he have to fight a giant serpent too?"

She looked at him. "Yes, though it was not so large; the giant Fafnir."

"How did he kill it?"

Together they changed direction, hoping to confuse the monster chasing them. "He lay in wait in the track it had hollowed out on the hill and struck when its heart was above him."

Kieth cursed. "It's too big for Gram to be able to pierce that far, and there's no track we can use anyway." He blinked furiously, fighting the red that was creeping around the edges of his vision. "What can we do?"

There was a sudden roar behind them. "I foundssss you!" Jörmungandr cried out, its head casting a shadow over them as it rose. They began to lunge to the side, only to be caught by its sweeping tail. Both went flying, Gram knocked loose from Solveig's hand. She crashed heavily against a tree trunk and crumbled to the group. Kieth landed with a splash in the river, breaking the ice on its surface.

He surfaced, sputtering wildly in the cold as he looked for Solveig. He found her lying next to the tree, her body limp, and Kieth's pulse quickened with fear. *No, NO!*

Jörmungandr cast about, searching for them with its one good eye. Black blood dripped from the other, mixing with its venom, and where it landed the trees and ground began to sizzle and smoke.

Kieth splashed out of the river, running to Solveig. He grabbed Gram from where it stuck up from the earth as he dashed past, dropping to his knees beside her. He panted, his body starting to shake, and realized as he groped for her wrist that he didn't have long left.

Kieth sighed in relief as he found a weak pulse, though one of her wings was obviously broken. "Stay here," he murmured, standing and uttering a quick prayer that Gram would work for him. He glanced at it, noting thankfully that while dimmed, its fire yet glowed.

Jörmungandr hissed in triumph as his gaze finally fell on the duo. It began to slither forward, confident that it had them dead to rights. Kieth looked at it, his blood rising as he thought of Solveig, in pain and unconscious; of the murder this creature had attempted and the fear it had spread for centuries prior; and lastly, of its father, Loki, and all of the evil he had done.

Kieth gripped Gram more tightly, the blade feeling familiar in his hand even though he had no idea how to use it. One thought remained with him as he surrendered the last shreds of his control – Solveig's comment of how Sigurðr had killed another serpent by piercing its heart.

What small corner of Kieth's mind retained sanity protested his quickly formed plan, but he ignored it, too consumed by his rage. As Jörmungandr leisurely opened its mouth wide, the fangs looking impossibly large this close to him, Kieth let out a roar and charged forward – and *into* the serpent's mouth.

Elena and Liam came to the frozen river that divided the islands. Liam eyed it nervously, jumping as Elena caught hold of his elbow. She snickered at him as she stepped up, walking a foot above the river and descending on the other side.

"Figured I wouldn't take any chances," she murmured as she released him. "Do you think they'll be okay?"

Liam shook his head. "I hope so – they're both great warriors, but… well. You saw the size of that thing."

She nodded. "It's strange, though; Jörmungandr was supposed to fight in Asgard. I can't imagine what it's doing here…"

He shrugged as they continued onward. "You'd know better than I. Anything from Loki?"

Elena frowned, concentrating for a moment. "I- I'm not sure. Just darkness, I think, and laughter, but it's hard to concentrate."

Liam looked at her worriedly. "Are you alright?"

She began to respond, stopping suddenly as a twig snapped somewhere ahead of them. "Did you hear that?" she breathed.

He too had frozen, Mjolnir in hand. Liam nodded, peering about. There was nothing to be seen, but he quietly pulled her to one side anyway, leading her towards a clearing dimly visible to their left. "We'll be able to see anything coming at us," he murmured.

Exiting the tree cover, they found themselves standing next to the river. A frozen waterfall hung over a rock face before them, and Liam felt something drawing him there. Elena seemed to feel the same way, taking his hand and pulling him towards it. Something else creaked within the forest, and they shot a nervous glance backwards before continuing.

Stepping to one side of the waterfall, Elena nodded in satisfaction at the sight of a darkened entrance. "I thought as much," she whispered, pulling him inside. "The cave Thor talked to the natives at – my dad brought me here once."

Liam followed her in, Mjolnir's glow giving them just enough light to see by. "I wonder," he said softly after a moment. "Thor and Kieth both said that the realms seemed closer here. Do you think that we could get to Asgard?"

She looked at him in surprise. "You want to help the gods," she murmured, realization dawning.

"I can't think of why else they'd have us here – and it definitely seems like they could use the help."

Elena frowned, thinking, but they were interrupted once more by a noise, this time a roar from outside. The duo hastened back to the entrance, Mjolnir's glow disappearing as if it sensed their need for stealth.

Outside stood half a dozen Jötun, three earth and three frost. They howled at one another, any spoken words indiscernible. Elena muttered a curse as one of the frost giants raised its head to the air, sniffing.

More grunts were exchanged, though now they seemed calmer, and the giants turned towards the island Solveig and Kieth were on.

"We have to stop them," Liam breathed, gripping his hammer more tightly. Elena grabbed his shoulder as he began to step forward, stopping him.

"Wait!" she hissed. "Let me. I've a better chance of outrunning them."

"We can take them," he replied. "I'm not letting you go alone."

She shook her head. "You should stay here, see if you can find a way to get to Asgard. Talk to Thor, maybe he can help – but I can't let them get to Kieth and Solveig." At his worried grimace she smiled, patting his shoulder. "Relax, I'm just going to lead them away. I'll see how much time I can buy you."

"Elena!" Liam caught her hand and she turned back to him, surprised. He searched for words, suddenly uncertain. "Just- come back quick, alright?"

She smiled. "Will do." She began to turn, but again he pulled her back.

Liam hesitated, fumbling with what he wanted to say. "Be careful, okay?" Tentatively he raised her hand, kissing the knuckles gently.

She laughed softly, blushing. "Pick that up from Thor?"

"That one's all me," he replied with a shy grin. She met his gaze, her eyes shining.

"You be careful too, alright?" She squeezed his hand. He nodded, his throat tight, and let her go, watching and waiting until she was out of sight before turning back to his search.

Within the great serpent was dark and moist, and Kieth's mind was suddenly glad that it was no longer in control as he rushed downward. He was dimly aware of Jörmungandr beginning to writhe and shake about, screaming, "It ticklesss! Sssstopsss it!"

Still roaring, Kieth continued forward, instincts guiding him as he raised Gram. His path was illuminated by the glow of the sword, and the blade began to hiss as it bit through the skin of the snake's throat. Thick blood began to drip as Jörmungandr's screams changed to ones of pain. Kieth paid no mind to the ichor that fell upon him.

He did not know how long he traveled, but at last he reached a point in the serpent where his mind bade him jump. His body fought the command for a moment until it realized that blood would be shed – only then did he lunge upwards, a wicked grin curving his lips.

The serpent shrieked, thrashing as Kieth began to hack with the sword. The weapon, once a tool of such grace and precision, was now reduced to being used as a machete cutting a path. Kieth lost track of which way was up and which was down, his mind focused on one simple task – blood. He did not notice when he chopped his way through a quickly pumping object – nor did he notice when his swings began to weaken, the venom that ran through the serpent's body beginning to slow him.

Kieth only paused when he emerged from the serpent itself into the cool night air, screaming his rage and pain to the sky as Jörmungandr thrashed weakly behind him in its death throes.

As the armies of the Jötun march towards us, even the bravest among us begin to shake. Though we do not stand alone - the forces of the Valkyr, the berserk, and the Einherjar behind us - the very footsteps of our enemies make the ground tremble.

A cry goes up from Njörðr along the coast, and I close my eyes as I hear his words. "The Naglfar! The dread ship is here!"

My father turns to the coast, and I feel myself calm at the sight of him. Even with the aura of battle tangible about us, he remains resolute. His white hair glows red in the light of the fire in the sky, and he looks like a young man once more. His single eye combs the Oceanside for sign of the ship, and I watch it widen as he stares.

"What is it?" I ask.

"Something is wrong!" he cries. "The captain – I cannot see him. Loki is not there!"

Elena ran in pursuit of the Jötun, shaking her head in an attempt to clear the growing darkness within it. She gained altitude as she ran, clearing the treetops and searching for the giants below her. It was the work of a moment for her to find them, aided as she was by the glow that they emanated.

As she drew closer to them Elena was struck by an idea. *Let's have a bit of fun,* she thought, grabbing a handful of snow from the treetops. Descending slightly, she waited until the last earth giant had walked past to fling the snow at it.

It let out a bellow of rage and whirled, stabbing the frost Jötun behind it before it could protest. The others likewise swung about, the frost giants roaring at the sight of their impaled companion. They leapt for the earth giant, whose two companions joined the melee in his defense.

Elena giggled from her vantage point, freezing as a dark voice purred, *Well done!* The realization of what she had done struck her, and she shook her head, groaning. The goal had been only to distract the giants – not to kill them!

She glanced back to the skirmish and found only one frost giant still standing. It was bloodied, though most of the blood dripped from its claws. The creature howled into the wind, its voice full of rage, pain, and sorrow, and Elena shivered. The darkness crept closer around her and she fled, leaving the creature to its own grief.

Liam cursed as he walked through the gate again, checking the rough stone walls once more for any sign of a gate. Mjolnir was glowing again, its pale blue light illuminating Liam's surroundings. "Bifrost?" he called tentatively, but there was no answer.

He grimaced, biting his lip. He had thought for sure that the gods would need his help, but it seemed as though he could not get to them. He turned back to the entrance, determined to go and help the others, and jumped as he saw Elena rounding a bend in the cave.

"Elena! Are you alright?"

She staggered slightly as he moved towards her, leaning heavily against the wall. "Liam…I don't feel so good," she murmured, suddenly collapsing.

He dashed towards her, yelling in surprise as Thor's voice suddenly filled the cave. *Liam! We've got a problem!*

"I'm a little busy!" he snarled.

You don't understand – Loki's dead!

Liam paused. "How is this a problem?"

Because he's not in Hel!

Elena looked up suddenly, and Liam froze at what he saw. Her pupils had expanded until her eyes were a solid, glistening black. When she spoke, it was not with her own voice. *"Hello, Thor. Did you miss me?"*

A sudden flood of darkness rushed out of her, slamming into Liam. He flew backwards through the frozen water spray, breaking the ice before landing heavily against a tree. His vision swam for a moment, clearing just in time for him to see Elena finish rising. Her normally graceful movements were jerky, something about the way her arms and legs moved not quite right.

Slowly she moved through the waterfall, dark laughter carrying to Liam's ears. *"And the mortal puppet, too – how nice. Now maybe we can all play together."*

Liam rose shakily, Mjolnir gripped tightly in his fist. "Let her go!"

"And why would I do that?" the voice asked, Elena's head cocking to one side. *"When I'm having so much fun?"*

Darkness rushed towards Liam again, but this time he was prepared, raising his hammer. The blue glow from it intensified, cutting through the black fog that rushed towards him. It flew past him on either side, and the weight of it staggered him – but he remained standing.

When he lowered Mjolnir Elena stood before him, backhanding him before he could move. The weight of the punch was more than she could have ever hoped to throw, and though Liam rolled with the blow he still found himself soaring across the river, landing heavily against another tree.

"Oh, this is enjoyable," the voice chuckled, moving leisurely towards Liam as he struggled to rise. *"You have no idea how much trouble you've caused me."*

"How are you here?" Liam forced out, wiping blood from his mouth. His head spun and he fought to focus as Elena began to skip. The sight was disturbing, her movements seeming forced as she walked atop the water. He noticed that her sandals now writhed with shadows, the material seeming to cling more tightly to her as tendrils of it moved up her legs.

"Oh, that's easy, my boy. You should know by now that we gods have a connection to the mortals we choose. I simply reinforced mine."

She paused a few feet before him, Liam staring up at her. He did not even try to stand, expecting to simply be thrown to the ground again. "I thought you were dead."

Loki laughed once more. *"My body is, no doubt. But that was all part of my brilliant plan – for you see, it was my body that kept me in place."* He seemed delighted to explain his scheme, and Liam was all too happy to keep him talking.

"You said you reinforced your bond – how?"

"Again – easy. I needed little enough energy in my own body to continue living, so I poured the rest into this mortal shell. It wasn't hard; a smidge here and there as she lay sleeping. I confess," he said, spinning about and looking

down, "*It isn't what I'm used to, but it shall do for now. Though she did provide a bit more of a challenge than I thought she would.*"

Liam felt his anger rise. "Damn right she did. Is she still in there?"

Her body quirked its head to one side as the god thought it over. "*I suppose,*" Loki said after a moment. "*Buried in some dark corner. I think I'll keep her there when I'm finished, maybe have some fun with her.*" He grinned wickedly.

Liam groaned. If there was even a chance that Elena was still alive, he couldn't risk hurting her – and he doubted he could do anything to Loki without harming her. An idea struck him and he raised Mjolnir, chucking lightning at the ground before her body.

Dirt and rocks flew, but Loki only laughed, raising Elena's hands as a shield of black fog thickened around her. Liam pushed himself to his feet only to be sent flying once more. This time he was able to roll with the impact, wobbling upright and bolting into the woods.

The myths he had read had said that both Loki and Jörmungandr were supposed to battle the gods – perhaps with them both on Midgard the Æsir would stand a chance. Maybe, just maybe, he could buy them time to win their battle – and then pray that they would be able to come and save *him*.

The battlefield is stained with carnage.

Crows circle overhead as our forces clash with those of the giants and the dead. To my right rears up the great wolf Fenrir, freed from his restraints by the shaking of the World Tree. My father and Viðarr stand in his path, struggling to hold him at bay from the rest of our army.

Farther away, near the Bifrost, I can see the ever-widening crack of the gate to Muspellheim. How the giants are opening the path is beyond my knowledge, but I know that we cannot hope to best their forces in our present state.

My mother rides towards me, and the gravity of the situation hits me. When even the gentle Frigg rides to battle…I shake my head, glad of the small break I have made in their forces. Without Mjolnir I am weaker than normal, but my lightning is still potent.

"My son," she calls out to me, pulling to a halt beside me. "Thor. Look at me. I know the decision you face."

I glance towards her. "Mother, please. I've made my choice – I will fight with my family, with my land."

She shakes her head sadly. "You do us proud, even without Mjolnir, but what of your friends? What of the mortals?" She holds her hand up for silence as I begin to speak. "Do not deny your friendship with them. I know as well as you the love that you have begun to foster for them. Look into your heart, my son; how do they fare?"

Grimacing, I peer within, and shock fills me at what I see. "Loki!" I cry out in rage. "He's on Midgard!"

Her face shows shock, but she masters her own feelings to aid me with mine. "You must help Liam, Thor – he cannot best Loki alone."

I nod, hugging her swiftly before tugging on my reigns. My loyal goats follow my lead, pulling my chariot towards the Bifrost. They take delight in stomping upon the corpses of the Jötun that already litter the field. As we ride I pray that I am not too late – and that the Bifrost yet stands. Hold on, Liam! *I send his way.*

Solveig opened her eyes groggily, wincing at the pain in her head. She gingerly raised a hand and felt her skull, grimacing at the sticky blood that coated it. The sight of it reminded her of what had happened, and she sat up too quickly. It took her a moment to force back the black spots that raced across her vision, and when she did she saw Jörmungandr lying not twenty feet from her, a pool of blood spilling from its mouth.

One of the bends of its body bore a gaping hole. With shock she saw a dark skinned body lying near the wound, her own flaming sword the only thing that drew her attention to it. She staggered upright, running as fast as she dared towards him with one wing dragging behind her on the ground. "Kieth!" she called out. "Kieth, no!"

She knelt over his shaking body, his skin and clothes stained dark with poisoned blood. He opened his eyes slowly, the last vestiges of red fading from his gaze at the sight of her face.

Kieth raised a trembling hand and gently touched her cheek, a soft smile on his face. "Don't cry," he murmured as he wiped away her tears. "I'm going to fight another battle."

She shook her head, sobbing. "I can't lose you," she cried. "I can't. Please, you can't die."

There was a soft fluttering of wings and a faint blue light began to glow behind her. Solveig spun around, a blood-drenched Gram in hand, and took up a defensive position. Before her stood a Valkyrie, dressed in a short tunic of mail and tall greaves. She wore a winged helm and bore a spear and shield, her wings luminescent with a pale blue sheen. "What are you doing here?" Solveig cried out. "You've got a battle to fight!"

The valkyr shook her head, her blue eyes pitying. "Our job remains; we go to collect the fallen and bring them home. We reinforce our ranks."

Solveig crouched, her sword raised. "Well, you cannot have this one. He is going to live!"

The woman's face was stern, though compassion showed in her gaze. "Sister, you know better than that. Feel within yourself – you know his time here is done." She paused, surveying Solveig. "And yours is almost done as well. The time for your choice is fast approaching."

Solveig's hair whipped about from the fury of her shaking head. "But my time is not come, and nor is his! You cannot have him!"

The valkyr sighed heavily, pulling off her helm and tossing her head as a mass of blonde hair fell. "Granddaughter, the choice I speak of may be closer than you think."

Solveig blinked. "Granddaughter – you are of my family?"

The woman smiled faintly. "My dear, I am the start of your family. I am Brynhildr."

"Brynhildr! Kieth, did you hear?" She turned back to the man only to find his eyes closed. His chest moved shallowly and she gasped, flinging herself to the ground near him. "Kieth, no!"

The valkyr moved closer to her. "Many things have the valkyr done for love of a mortal – I know this as well as anyone. There is a sacrifice you may make that could save him."

Solveig looked up at her. "Anything."

Her ancestor knelt beside her. "You have used much of your powers, and soon must choose to become either a mortal or a Valkyrie. Either choice requires a sacrifice of half of your life – but what few know is that this life may be gifted to another."

Kieth's pulse slowed further beneath Solveig's fingertips, and she felt her own heart stop for a moment as his skipped a beat. Brynhildr continued, "You may choose to let him die and yourself become a valkyr, serving him eternally in Asgard where he shall never know sorrow, only the joy of combat and companionship – or, you may choose to become a valkyr and heal him, allowing him to lead his own life on Midgard as you watch on from Valhalla."

"Or," she added, her voice soft, "You may choose to give up your powers and become a mortal, saving him in the process so that the two of you may lead a normal life – at least, as normal as a berserk's life can be."

The older valkyr watched her for a moment as Solveig gazed at Kieth. The lifkyr sighed, her breath hitching. "It was no coincidence that it was you who came, was it, Grandmother?"

The valkyrie shook her head. "I rarely leave Valhalla now. It was Odin who told me to come – he thought the choice would be best given by family."

Solveig was slow to answer, but when she spoke, her words were sure. "There is still a battle to be fought. I will rise to Valhalla – and so will he. It's what he would want."

A breeze began to pick up as Brynhildr nodded, her smile sad. "So be it, child. We will meet again soon."

The wind rose and a thick purple glow surrounded Solveig. She felt the life leave Kieth's body and fought a sob as she stood, radiating violet light. It grew until she was blinded by it, the glow becoming all that she could see, and she blinked hastily in an attempt to clear her vision.

Merciful darkness suddenly enveloped her face, though a tee of bright amethyst remained. She raised a gloved hand to her face and found it covered with a steel helm, engraved wings rising from her temples. The light slowly faded until she could see the inside of a hall lit by torches, the floor strewn with fur rugs and pelts. A long table filled the center of the hall, benches shoved back and some knocked over from the haste with which they had been moved.

Solveig rolled her shoulders and heard the chink of mail. She nodded slowly and began to move, looking for Kieth.

Kieth opened his eyes slowly. A silvery colored blur before him solidified into Solveig, who stared at him worriedly. "Kieth? Are you awake?"

He blinked, sitting up. Something told him that he should be feeling pain, but there was nothing – he felt as though he had awakened from a long sleep. "Where are we?"

She bit her lip and his gaze traveled down her, taking in the armor that she bore. She seemed older, somehow, and the torchlight that lit her face brought out a more feral aspect. She brushed back her curtain of hair and he decided that the look suited her.

His eyes widened as she finally responded. "Valhalla."

Her hand clutched the gold trimmed helm in her hand as she awaited his response. It took him a moment to gather his thoughts. "Then...I'm dead, right?"

Solveig let out a soft laugh. "After a fashion."

"And you?" He reached out a hand, touching her cheek gently. "Lord forgive me, I thought I'd slain the beast. I'd hoped to spare you this."

She shook her head fiercely, wrapping his hand in her own. "Don't. You did stop him – this was my choice. I could not let you fight this battle alone."

Kieth's vision swam for a moment and he closed his eyes, his emotions roiling. It was a moment before he opened them, and when he spoke his voice was thick. "I- there are no words, Solveig. Thank you. But you're right – we're not done yet. Where do we go from here?"

She stood, helping him to his feet, and it was only then that Kieth noticed his own garments. He was clothed as a berserk of old, dressed in leather and mail with a thick bear skin thrown over his shoulders. A sword and shield lay to his side and at his feet, and he bent to grab them. They fit as though made for him – and he rather suspected that they had been.

When he looked back up Solveig had donned her helm, her hair piled inside it. She drew her sword from its sheathe, and Kieth was glad to see that she still bore Gram. Together they stepped outside, and in the flickering torchlight they were met with a grateful whinny.

Gunnar pranced over from the grass that lay outside the hall, nuzzling both of them. Solveig murmured to him for a moment before mounting, reaching out a hand for Kieth. He smiled grimly at her as he took it, clambering onto the horse behind her. "Let's go win this war."

The battlefield was chaos.

It hadn't been hard to find – the army of the Æsir had left tracks that were easy to follow even in the dark of the unnatural night. Their way was lit by the red crack in the sky, which appeared even closer in Asgard. As they traveled onward, Gunnar galloping across the sky, they saw more fires up ahead.

Up close the din of combat was nearly deafening, and the sight was beyond description. Kieth felt Solveig shift before him, eyeing the battle in an attempt to distinguish sides. He held her a little tighter as he too looked, their overhead vantage point allowing them an eagle eye view.

Though there had no doubt been ranks and lines at one point, they had crumpled beneath the mass of the opposing forces. Whatever grass the plains had once borne had been trampled beneath the feet of the two armies, and they swirled in chaos.

The giants were easy to mark – their tribal tattoos glowed bright in the darkness, though frost and earth seemed to be jumbled together. They fought in small clusters against the shining steel, bronze, and gold of those that the duo took to be the Æsir's forces, though it was difficult to tell.

As they rode overhead the coast came into sight, presenting an entirely new landscape. Though a few of the Jötun yet fought here, for the most part the forces opposing the gods were clothed in black. The stench of decay was potent even from the air, signaling that these were the forces of the dead.

Upon the beach itself was anchored a terrible ship. It was a pale and sickly gray color, standing out starkly against the dark landscape. Kieth's stomach turned as they rode closer. "I thought the Nail ship was a myth," he shouted, trying to be heard over the din of battle.

"Nailfarer Naglfar." Solveig grimaced. "I'd hoped the tales of a ship made of fingernails were exaggerated."

They circled, Solveig trying to find a place to safely dismount where they could make an impact on the battle. New horrors met them as they rode on, and both flinched as a soul-shaking howl split the sky. Gunnar reared, the motion terrifying in the open air, but the duo managed to keep their seats.

Below them stood a gigantic wolf, his gray fur matted. He loped through the battlefield, scattering or crushing those below him without seeming to care which side they were on. None could stand before him, though a few seemed determined to try.

Before the wolf stood a shining golden chariot. The horses that pulled it shied as the wolf bounded nearer, but the man who held their reins stood resolute. Those around him scattered as the wolf pounced, landing with his tail up and his head close to the ground before the chariot.

The wolf howled again, but this time Solveig kept a tight grip on the reigns. She began to descend, Gunnar reluctantly obeying her, but the horse suddenly shied at a black shadow that swooped before him.

Kieth drew his sword one handed and prepared to fight as the shadow curved towards him, but Solveig stayed his hand. The shadow solidified into a raven that perched on the end of his sword, looking at him with eyes that seemed almost human.

Both jumped as it spoke, vaguely aware of the wolf and chariot that circled one another below them. "This battle is not for you, brave ones. My lord can handle Fenrir – you are needed at the Bifrost."

Solveig glanced below, all of the tales she had read of Odin's defeat at the paw of the wolf flashing through her mind. The raven studied her, and she finally nodded grimly. "I will trust that the All-father has a plan. Which way?"

"Follow me!" the bird cawed, flapping its wings once more. It wheeled away more swiftly than they could have imagined. They reluctantly followed, Solveig's mouth closed in a grim slash as they left Odin to his fate.

The snarls of Fenrir could still be heard behind them as the raven slowed. It hovered for a moment, its beak pointing towards a hill that seemed largely untouched by the battle. "That way!" it called out. "Should Surtr and the fire Jötun join this battle, it will mean our end. You must hold them!" The bird wheeled away suddenly, soaring back towards the battlefield.

"Hold them until what?" Kieth yelled, but it was too late.

Solveig breathed a curse as she descended, making for the tall stone block that rested atop the hill. The shadow of the great stone stretched out over those that stood near it. The red chasm in the sky grew slowly but steadily behind it, flinging out enough fiery light to illuminate the hilltop.

As they landed and dismounted Kieth and Solveig saw that the stone was carved with runes similar to those on the gate to the Norns. Faint light in every color of the rainbow played through the cracks etched into the rock, a sight that Kieth aptly described as "Trippy."

The man that stood behind them barked out a laugh at the term. He stepped towards them as Solveig finished murmuring to Gunnar and sent him galloping off with a slap to the rump, unwilling to keep him close when combat seemed likely.

Kieth nodded to the man who approached him. He was like nothing either had ever seen before, with skin so white that it seemed to shine in the darkness and teeth that flashed gold when he smiled at them. The gold matched his gleaming armor. A great horn was slung over one shoulder, hanging from a baldric. "Good to see Odin found us some backup. I am Heimdallr."

They nodded at him as another man stepped forward, conspicuous in his lack of weapons. He too was armored in plate, though his shone like steel. His golden hair fell gleaming to his shoulders where it merged with his fair, bushy beard. Blue eyes sparkled as he bowed to Solveig, nodding at Kieth. "Well met, friends. I am Freyr."

The duo introduced themselves. The pleasantries exchanged, Kieth went to business. "Has no one come through the gate?"

The two gods exchanged looks. "Thor went through several minutes ago," Heimdallr explained, "But no one has entered Asgard yet."

"No thing might be a better term," Freyr added grimly. "But the crack is spreading and the Bifrost is beginning to light up. It is simply a matter of time now."

Solveig looked about the hilltop, which stood empty save for the four of them. "Does no one stand with us?"

They shook their heads. "Our forces were needed elsewhere – Heimdallr should not even be here."

"And Loki should have been with the ship," the big man growled. "We have covered this, Freyr – since he was not, I stand here. I *am* the guardian of the Bifrost, after all."

Freyr sighed as Kieth and Solveig looked at one another. "You mean Loki didn't captain the ship?" Kieth asked.

"He never showed. I dread to think what mischief he might be causing, though I can hope the quake crushed him beneath a mound of rubble." Freyr grinned cheerfully at the thought, though Heimdallr looked as though he shared their concern.

"But I do not mind a little company," the god continued, his voice cheerful. "And honestly, it will not take many to hold the Bifrost. The giants can only send so many through at a time."

Heimdallr shook his head. "But they *can* breathe fire."

Freyr shrugged. "Only if we give them time to."

Kieth and Solveig locked eyes again, struck by the youthful enthusiasm of the fertility god. Heimdallr seemed more experienced with combat, but they were left to wonder how effective their small group would be at holding the bridge. Having nothing to do but wait, they turned and gazed out at the battle that played below their feet as the gods clashed against the forces of Hel.

Solveig had only just caved in to fatigue and sat in the tall grass when the gate exploded with rainbow light. "Here they come!" Heimdallr roared as he drew his huge two-handed sword. Kieth cursed as he helped Solveig to her feet, both of them reaching for their own blades.

The only warning they had was the sudden burst of hot air that seared through the open Bifrost. From the rainbow descended the fire Jötun of Muspellheim, charging out two at a time and roaring their fury to the darkened skies.

Solveig and Kieth saw only flashes of the giants as they closed for combat. Like their frost and hill brethren, they were enormous. Easily ten feet tall, even with their hunched backs, they towered over the gods. Red flaming tattoos were carved into their very flesh, the light illuminating the battlefield. The reek of burning skin was sickening.

Solveig darted forward with her own burning blade, crying out as she slashed at her opponent. He lunged for her with teeth filed into points and lost his head for his trouble as she continued onward.

Kieth roared as he swung at his foe, the sword light as a feather in his hands. It shattered the giant's bone spear, continuing through to deliver a mortal blow to its stomach. Kieth fought the rage he felt pressing in on him, struggling to hold on for as long as he could, and turned to find another Jötun.

But no matter how well the duo fought, they could not hope to compare to the Æsir.

Heimdallr and Freyr stood side by side before the gate, with just enough room to either side of them to allow a few lone giants to charge past and be met by Kieth and Solveig. The gods held their line, meeting the Jötun calmly and dispatching them with nonchalance. The Watcher swung his sword with control, taking care not to overextend himself. Those that made it past him were met by Freyr's bare hands, the god roaring his own battlecry as he snapped necks and crushed bones with backhanded blows.

The very hill itself seemed to rise up against the invaders as the four fought on. Tall grass and what seemed to be wheat rose around them at Freyr's command, tangling itself amongst the Jötun, and though the grass burned it served to slow the giants.

Solveig saw Kieth suddenly hurl his shield at a charging giant, bowling him over with the strength of the blow. The berserk howled in triumph as he fell upon a tripped Jötun, beating at it indiscriminately with the blade *and* the flat of his sword. Another of the fire giants closed with Solveig and she lunged for him, losing track of the others for a moment.

The battle grew more frenzied, and she saw only glimpses of her comrades. Here was Heimdallr, still standing in the same place, his face alight with fearsome laughter as he dispatched his enemy. And there was Freyr, one hand clutching a giant's throat as the other extended to a Jötun tangled in crops. The god's eyes glowed with an eerie light as the wheat billowed in a path from his hand, choking the Jötun as it shoved itself down the giant's throat. She saw Kieth tackle another giant, roaring with pain as his hands closed about its fiery skin - but he held on despite the pain, bearing it to the ground.

Solveig could not have said how long they fought, but there came a time when the battle lulled and she was able to stop and catch her breath. Experience told her that she should have been bone weary, but the ache in her arms was sweet and her pulse remained almost normal – perhaps a side effect of her ascension to Valhalla.

She looked to the portal where the giants were now coming through more cautiously, seeming to have learned from their fallen comrades. The hilltop was

98

littered with the corpses of their brethren, hindering Heimdallr and Freyr's attacks. She moved hastily to clear some of the bodies as Kieth fell to his knees, panting as he tried to regain control.

Solveig had come within ten feet of the gate itself when the battle changed. A blast of scalding air swept from the Bifrost entry, blowing everyone off of their feet and down the hill. What giants were left alive grinned manically, their eyes alight with a strange combination of exultation and terror.

A fresh roar sent another blast of air through the gate, followed by a voice that seared Solveig's ears as it crackled over the hilltop. *"I COME!"*

What burst through the entry to the rainbow bridge was as similar to the fire Jötun as a chihuahua is to a wolf. The head came through first, followed slowly by the rest of the monster, its body bent almost double as it squeezed itself through the portal.

Solveig struggled upright, staring. The creature's feet were enormous, each bearing three long, pointed obsidian claws that sparkled with what seemed to be filings from the Bifrost – indeed, she could hear the bridge creaking from the weight and sheer heat of those that walked upon it.

Her gaze traveled up the monstrosity. Its burgundy body was awash with a fiery light. The tattoos upon it were more elaborate than those upon the Jötun who had come before, and seemed to be carved deeper. Red flames gushed from the markings, the very lifeblood of the creature serving as a weapon against its foes. Lava dripped from the marks over the bulging muscles of the legs, interrupted on each knobby kneecap by a sharp bone spur that curved to the middle of its thigh.

The creature, whom she deemed to be Surtr, ruler of Muspellheim, was clothed only in a loincloth. The garment was made of a red silk that glowed and shifted like the fires Surtr wore as a second skin. His chest was thick, even for a being so tall, his shoulders broad with hulking thews. Pointed bone spurs jutted out from his elbows as well, and Solveig noted dimly that in one of his three fingered hands Surtr bore a flaming sword – though it was considerably larger than her own.

It was his face that was the real horror, though, perched atop of a thick, short neck. Bones poked out from his chin and the ridge of his eyebrows, and huge, curling horns of black rose from above his pointed ears. Surtr's hair was a mane of fire that crackled and seethed as he stepped forward, the ground shaking from his weight as Freyr's plants singed and wilted around the beast.

"ÆSIR," he hissed, and Freyr fell to the ground screaming and clutching his ears as the grasses on the hilltop burst into sudden flames. The others trembled before the Jötun, and Solveig felt a trickle of wetness run down her cheek as her ears began to bleed. Kieth clutched his head as the voice strove to split his skull, crawling towards Solveig. Some portion of his mind that wasn't cowering noted that Heimdallr was nowhere to be seen as Surtr continued,

"AND MORTALS, TOO – HOW KIND OF YOU TO PREPARE ME A SNACK!"

The Jötun reached out a hand for Freyr, the god struggling to move from Surtr's path while in obvious agony. The fire that emanated from the giant was suddenly reflected by something that shone gold. Heimdallr leapt from the top of the stone gate itself, somehow having managed to scale the back in the confusion. His sword clove down with the full weight of his momentum into Surtr's back and the giant screamed as it bit into his flesh. Heimdallr's roar of pain as scalding blood sprayed onto him could barely be heard over the sheer volume of Surtr's lungs.

The giant whirled with more speed than anything its size had any right to have, backhanding Heimdallr through the Bifrost portal. The Watcher disappeared into the rainbow mists, but he had bought enough time for the others to rally to their feet.

They noticed with despair that the wound Heimdallr had caused was already closed, the sheer heat of the monster cauterizing the injury almost immediately. Heimdallr's sword lay smoking down the hillside, the blade warped and distended from the furnace-like temperatures.

Surtr laughed at their despair. *"YOUR END IS COME, PUNY GODS! NOW BEGINS A NEW AGE…THE AGE OF FIRE!"*

Kieth met Solveig's eyes through the flame, and she nodded to him. Together they raised their swords, battle cries ripping from their throats-

-only to stare in shock as a frost Jötun charged past them and tackled Surtr. He was large for a Jötun, though tiny in comparison to Surtr. If the myths were true and the size of a Jötun's horns told their age, then he was ancient. Magnificent horns that curled like a ram's sprouted from his forehead, the points dragging against his shoulders. His mane was a frozen waterfall, his teeth and claws icicles, and he put them to good use.

Steam exploded outward from the melee as frost met fire. Kieth threw himself over where Freyr lay twitching on the ground, shielding the god as he and Solveig dragged him away from the killzone.

They watched the fight in awe. The smaller giant used his speed and size to his advantage, always one step ahead of Surtr. Still, he was slowing, and the duo readied themselves to fight once more.

The old frost giant finally slipped up, dodging a split second too slowly. Surtr seized him by the leg and raised him with a roar of triumph, preparing to split him in two.

There was no warning before a small army of frost and earth Jötun charged past and into the fray, all significantly smaller and younger than the first. They swarmed Surtr, using their numbers against him. He growled, making the hill rumble, unable to both fight them off and dispatch the old frost Jötun. With a roar he threw the frost giant down the hill, freeing his hands to deal with the others.

Kieth looked at Solveig, who nodded. "Stay with Freyr, I'll check on the giant," he murmured as he stood, but an icy hand stopped him.

Solveig reached for her sword, hesitant to attack the Jötun that backed away from Kieth, its hands raised in submission. "Peace, warriors," it growled as Kieth turned, and the duo recognized it as the ancient one who had attack Surtr, somehow on his feet once more. "This fight is not for you."

The berserk and the valkyr exchanged glances. "I don't understand-" Kieth began,

The old giant raised his hand as he eyed the battle. "If the heat did not kill you, the frost or the earth would. We have prepared for this fight for millennia. You must not interfere."

He glanced back at them, a cold gleam in his eye stopping their protests. "Watch," he growled, "And tend to your wounded."

After a moment they reluctantly turned to Freyr, forced to concede the giant's point. Solveig tried to patch the god's wounds, doing her best to keep him comfortable as Kieth watched over them.

More and more Jötun swarmed past, the battlefield below changing as the forces of the gods realized that not all of the Jötun were enemies. At the top of the hill, the giants climbed over one another to reach Surtr, the ancient frost giant bellowing commands from the hillside.

Steam rose as frost giants flung themselves onto fire. Earth Jötun hardened their skin to stone and dirt and worked to smother the flames. Surtr's roars turned from annoyance to agony as more Jötun joined the battle. Some stood to the side, earth and frost working together to send jets of water to extinguish the fires and vines to trip the great Jötun.

The shockwave when they succeeded knocked both sides of the battle to the ground and cracked the stone gate of the Bifrost. Surtr's cries began to change pitch, from the crackling of an open flame to the high whistle of a teapot. The old frost Jötun once more threw himself into the battle, leading the rest of his forces with him.

Solveig called a warning as a dark shape swooped for Kieth, and he turned to find the raven hovering beside him. "The All-father says you must run," it panted. Noting its missing feathers, Kieth offered a shoulder, which it gratefully latched onto. Together he and Solveig hauled an incoherent Freyr to his feet, the group stumbling down the hillside.

They barely made it. The raven let out a shrill screech and flapped its wings, the small movement somehow summoning a wave of air that knocked them all to the ground. There was a moment of eerie silence, and then a deafening wave of hot air slammed overhead as Surtr seemed to combust. The wave flung back those who still stood on the hill, knocking them all to the ground.

Liam paused and leaned heavily against a tree, panting for breath. He had circled around from where he had begun, and once again stood a short distance from the cave. After a moment he straightened, listening for any sign of pursuit. The forest was eerily silent, and he groaned. He had wanted to keep ahead of Loki, not to lose him entirely. Now the god might go after the others.

Liam took one last deep breath before rounding the tree, heading back the way he had come. He found his path blocked by a dark shadow that solidified into Elena.

"*Found you!*" Loki crowed, backhanding Liam again. He felt his nose break as he fell backwards, struggling to twist into a roll. He succeeded only partially and felt his ribs creak from the strain. Rising as quickly as he could and forcing back the pain from his many scrapes and bruises, Liam groaned to see Elena standing in front of him.

"*I must confess, I'm growing tired of hide and seek,*" the god whispered malevolently, extending a hand as Liam tried to dodge. Elena's body seized him by his collar, slamming him into a tree and raising him until his feet dangled a foot above the ground. "*Aren't you?*"

Liam struggled, unable to get the leverage to fight back – and he suspected that he wouldn't do much damage even if he *could* hit the god. Loki possessed a superhuman level of strength – which fit, Liam supposed, since the god wasn't human.

Elena grabbed Liam's wrist with her other hand, shoving it backwards and tightening her grip until he felt his fingers growing numb. Still he held onto Mjolnir, secure in the knowledge that dropping it would be a *very* bad idea.

"I'll ask you one more time," he panted at Loki, whose eyebrows raised in puzzlement. "Let her go."

The god laughed, and Liam was grateful for whatever time his comment had bought. *Thor! Tell me you guys are winning!*

It was a moment before the god responded, obviously distracted by something. Liam heard a bit of Loki's rant about his ingenious plan, ignoring most of it as he waited. *Liam? Are you alright?*

Define alright! he yelled back. *I thought you said he was dead!*

His body, yes! I- listen to what he's saying!

Liam tuned back in to Loki waxing eloquent about his plot. "*You see, the myths always said that the earthquake would free me – but never how. It wasn't hard to realize that I was not going to survive physically, and I had better things to do in the afterlife than captain a crew of misbegotten fools to conquer Asgard. Besides, as everyone knows, that tale ends in death for all. But on Midgard – well. Let's just say that this realm has always had a plethora of possibilities.*"

Is there any way to stop him without hurting Elena? Liam asked.

Thor was silent for a moment. *If he truly is dead, then only the Æsir and their relics may harm him now. I can't say for sure if that would affect her or not.*

Then we don't do it, Liam replied, his voice firm.

Loki suddenly dropped him and Liam landed heavily, his attention snapping back to the evil god's words. *"I will rise up and rule this realm as god, as it always should have been! No pantheon, no meddling Odin, no one to split the worship with. I, and I alone, will bring this realm to its knees – and I think I'll start with you! Now, kneel before your new god!"*

Elena flung her hand outward, and an unseen pressure shoved Liam steadily downward despite his efforts. Liam grimaced in pain, his hand rising to clutch his cross necklace. Uttering a silent prayer, he struggled to his feet, Mjolnir held tight in his hand though he had lost all feeling in it. "I bow before *one* God," he forced out, swinging the hammer upwards to combat the dark.

The blue light cut through the swath of darkness, shoving Loki back. Elena's face contorted in a grimace. Her hands rose up defensively, driving Liam backwards. Blue and black energy seethed between them, crackling as it expanded.

Hold on! Liam dimly heard Thor plead. *I'm almost there!*

There was a sudden explosion of light, the combating magics too powerful to sustain for long. The ground between Liam and Elena exploded, sending both flying backwards. Liam hit the ground and felt his wrist snap as he landed wrong, his head bouncing off of the packed snow and dirt. Black spots swam around his vision.

He blinked heavily, finally managing to drive the spots back, and found himself staring into Loki's eerie black eyes. *"If you will not kneel, then you shall die,"* the god hissed, his eyes flashing as he continued their conversation as though it had never been interrupted.

Elena's hand rose, shadows running up and down its length and solidifying into a black spear. With a cry Loki drove it towards Liam, who raised his hammer a heartbeat too slowly in defense –

Only to find the spear stopped a handbreadth away from his heart.

Elena's body shook as her head turned to stare at the spear in shock. Her mouth moved, and Liam's heart jumped for joy at the sound of her own voice.

"You will not touch him!" she shouted, and flung herself backwards. She fell, her hands extending at the last possibly moment to break her fall. Liam pushed himself upright, crying out in pain as his weight fell temporarily on his injured wrist.

"Impossible!" Loki shrieked, struggling to rise. The sight was strange, as half of Elena's body fought to do his will, the other her own. The god roared with rage, raising her hands to her face. After a moment she slid them down her neck as Liam struggled towards them.

"*Mine again,*" Loki murmured, flinging out a hand that sent Liam flying through the air once more. He crashed into what remained of the icicles that were the waterfall and found himself lying on the cave floor again.

Loki staggered through the cave entrance, hindered by Elena's hands that clawed at the walls. "Liam!" she yelled. "Use the hammer, just do it-"

The god shrieked in an ancient black tongue, the words echoing through the cave like thunder, and Liam felt his skin crawl at the sound of them as he forced himself to rise onto one knee. "*No more of that,*" Loki muttered after a moment, his eyes flashing in triumph. "*Now, where were we?*"

He began to move forward, and Liam finally heard the voice he'd been waiting for. *Elena!* cried Thor, and Liam suddenly felt his presence, stronger than ever before. Emotions flashed through his mind that were not his own – regret and worry at being so late, fear for Elena and what Loki might have done to her, and outrage focused on the trickster god himself.

"Elena!" Liam shouted as well. "You've got to hold on!" *Help me, Thor!*

As Loki stepped forward, his path unsteady as though struggling to control a puppet, Liam was blinded by a flash of lightning. It seemed to center on him, the blast radius flinging Loki and Elena several feet back. Liam was dimly aware of Thor's voice in the background, thundering, *I will NOT let you hurt my friends!*

Elena sat up jerkily, her mouth curved in a snarl. She stood, and it was Loki's laughter that emanated from her lips, dark and twisted. Liam flinched as Thor's voice seemed to come from right next to him. *What would you give to protect her?* the god asked rapidly.

Anything, he replied silently. *Anything at all.*

Loki's voice was harsh, sounding profoundly wrong as it came form Elena. "*And what do you think you can do? Who do you think you are, to try and stop ME?*"

Liam's grip tightened on Mjolnir, the handle feeling as though it had been made for him. He felt Thor guiding him as never before, the god's thoughts barely communicated before being acted upon by Liam. His gray eyes flashed as sparks ran up and down his body, playing through his hair and beard. When he spoke, it was with two voices seamlessly merged into one.

"*I am Thor,*" they replied, and as Loki's eyes widened they raised their hammer. They swung, aiming for the ground beneath her feet, and Elena's legs were swept out from under her with the ensuing explosion of stone.

Loki began to crawl backwards. "*Impossible! You were to fight with the rest of the gods!*" he shrieked.

Thor shrugged, Liam's shoulders rolling. "***Times change, fiend – you were the one who changed them. It's time you caught up.***"

They raised their hammer, feeling it shift to accommodate their wishes as it rose. By the time it reached eye level it was once more Liam's faithful .45, the grip resting securely in their hand. Loki thrashed about, desperately trying to escape, but seemed held fast – Liam suspected by Elena.

He uttered a quick prayer that Thor's theory was correct as they pulled the trigger, sending thunder echoing through the cavern after a brilliant flash of blinding light.

When Kieth opened his eyes Odin stood before him, hands extended to pull he and Solveig to their feet. The god was covered in blood and sweat, his beard and hair matted, but his eye twinkled and his grip was steady.

"What- what happened?" Solveig asked.

He smiled, his gaze traveling to beyond her. "We won, my dear."

A weary chuckle came from behind the duo, and they turned to find the old frost Jötun leaning on a younger warrior, his forces gathered behind him. "All-father," he murmured.

"I don't understand," Kieth frowned. "Why help us? Why change sides?"

The Jötun shook his head. "Not all of us long for the end of the Tree, berserk. It would mean our end as well."

The other giants nodded as he continued, though many looked ready to collapse. "Your people are not the only ones with prophecies. We knew this day would come, and have waited for countless time to prevent it, outcasts among our own people. Though many of us did not survive the battle, our task is complete – we may rest in peace."

Odin stepped forward, both sides wary as the odd duo looked at one another. Hands fell to weapons as the All-father clapped the Jötun's arm, but the old giant waved them down.

"They will not be forgotten, my friend," Odin said softly. "If you will give me their names, I shall raise a monument on this site to their bravery."

The giant seemed to like that, though he still spoke with caution. "I am not sure we may be counted friends, All-father. There have been many wrongs done by both sides, grievances that are hard to forget."

Odin nodded. "Aye. But for today, let us put that aside. Please, allow us to tend to your wounded – though it is too little thanks by far for your actions today."

The Jötun hesitated for a moment, glancing back at his forces before grasping the All-father's hand. "It would be appreciated," he admitted wearily.

When Liam's vision cleared he found Loki lying against the remnants of a shattered tree, unconscious from the force of his collision with both it and the stone of the cave that was now shattered into a new entrance. A smoking, cauterized hole marred his chest, though no scent of burning flesh reached Liam's nose. The god appeared as he had in Liam's dreams – thin and wiry with long, straight black hair and an angular face – and though his eyes were closed, Liam felt sure they would be as black as they had looked on Elena.

He dismissed the god, turning and searching for the librarian, terrified of what he might find. His gaze fell on her moments later, draped across the ground where she had stood before, trapped in a deep sleep. Liam knelt beside her, feeling a soft tugging on his mind that he ignored. Checking desperately for a pulse, he uttered a sigh of relief when he found a faint one.

"Liam," murmured Thor, and it took him a moment to realize that the voice had not come from within. Glancing to his side in shock, Liam saw the god kneeling beside him. His eyes were grave, his beard wild, and Liam felt the full weight of his attention like a clap of thunder.

"How – what are you doing here?" Liam asked.

Thor shook his head. "There is little time. She's fading fast – Loki drew upon much of her life force to be able to enter this realm. She is falling into the spirit world herself, and unless she has something to hold onto, I doubt that we'll be able to stop it."

Liam shook his head. "No. No, she stays here." He bent over Elena, picking her up and cradling her against his chest. "Elena, can you hear me?" he murmured, rocking her. Thor stepped back to give them space, frowning as he turned to Loki.

"You have to hang in there. It's over – we've won. The doom is delayed because of you; you saved Thor and I. You have to stay."

There was no answer, and Liam noted with worry that her skin was growing paler – and colder. "Elena, come on. Your family needs you – your father! You have to see him through this."

Still nothing. Liam's heart raced as her own slowed, and he glanced at Thor in panic. The god turned as though he had felt Liam's gaze, shaking his head sadly. "There is nothing *I* can say," he murmured, his quiet words somehow carrying over the distance.

Liam shook his head, returning his attention to the raven-haired woman in his arms. He grabbed her hand, holding it tight. "Elena," he whispered, cradling her closer. "If you die, I'm coming to Valhalla to get you back. I won't leave you there alone, do you hear me?" He closed his eyes, burying his face in her hair as the tears started. "Please. Please, I think I'm falling in love with you."

For a moment time stood still, the only sound Liam's pounding heart. Then Elena drew in a deep breath, her chest swelling as her hand tightened almost imperceptibly around his. Liam let out a breath he had not known he had held as she simply breathed for a moment, her warmth rapidly returning as Liam rocked her.

As her eyes opened groggily he heard Loki shriek, looking back to find the god apparently conscious enough to feel panic. He struggled to rise, his black eyes focused on Elena with murderous intent, but Thor stood between them. The god of thunder stepped forward, Mjolnir in hand, and grabbed Loki's neck with one hand. Grimly he shoved him into anther tree – or tried to, finding that the mischief-maker passed right through it.

Thor shook his head, pulling Loki back. "It appears you are no longer welcome in this realm," he said with a grin, his grip tightening. "Let's take you home, shall we? I'm sure your dear little pet snake has missed you. Bifrost!" he called out.

Loki screamed as the rainbow light began to appear. Though dimmer and thinner than normal, the bridge nonetheless stood firm, and Liam smiled to see it. Thor turned before he stepped onto the bridge, tossing his hammer towards Liam. "I'll be back for that," he called, holding Loki at arm's length as he strode out of sight along the bridge.

Liam shook his head and looked back at Elena, only to find her eyes focused on his face. He blinked. "Hi," she murmured.

"Heh. Hi," he replied, returning her gaze.

She grimaced suddenly as her eyes dropped to his wrist, twisted at an unnatural angle on the ground next to her. "Oh, crows! That was me, wasn't it?"

"Not exactly," Liam said with a laugh. "In fact, I think I should thank you for it not being worse."

Jötun and Æsir worked together to gather the injured from the battlefield. Odin called for volunteers to go through the Bifrost to find its guardian and seemed unsurprised when Kieth and Solveig stood.

Though obviously damaged, the gates yet stood, and the bridge seemed sturdy enough as they walked out onto it. The sight that met them made Kieth roar with laughter.

Several yards away Heimdallr was being helped to his feet by a red-headed man who held a writhing serpent in one fist. A pile of Jötun corpses stretched out behind them, some barely on the bridge – which, though cracked and dim, held strong beneath their feet.

Heimdallr rose unsteadily, one of the Jötun's blades still gripped in his hand. The left side of his face was covered in a sheet of blood, a stark contrast to his white skin, but he seemed in good spirits. His teeth flashed in a golden grin as the duo approached.

"I found a better place to hold them," he called, and the man who stood with him laughed.

"You must be Thor," Kieth said as Solveig ducked beneath the Watcher's arm, bracing him.

"Must be?" the stranger replied, one eyebrow arched.

"You look like Liam," the valkyr replied, and the god grinned.

"I rather think that it's he who looks like me, but that is a moot point. What news from beyond the gate?"

"I'll let you hear it from your father," Kieth said, smiling at Thor's obvious relief to hear that Odin yet lived. Together the four headed back, wading through the corpses of the Jötun Heimdallr had cut down.

The gatekeeper was left with the healers, and the remaining trio went to find Odin. He excused himself from his conversation with the old frost giant at the sight of his son, enveloping him in a huge hug. They had a quick whispered conversation about the snake that now hung limp in Thor's hand before Odin gingerly took it from him.

"You could have left him *some* air," the All-father scolded.

The god of thunder shrugged, offering his father an unrepentant grin. Odin shook his head and held up the snake, allowing the two ravens that followed him to grasp it and fly off. They all watched it for a moment before Thor cleared his throat.

"Father," he asked, "Why are there Jötun everywhere?" He seemed confused at the laughter that followed his question.

Tales were exchanged, and in the silence afterward Odin stood thinking. He glanced at Kieth and the berserk bit his lip, wondering what he had done.

The All-father offered him a sad smile. "You'll want to see your friends, I imagine. Midgard is lost to you, but you may yet set foot on the Bifrost. Thor, kindly gather Liam and Elena – I'll see what I can do to retrieve Mjolnir later."

Kieth blinked as Thor nodded, boarding a cart that was inexplicably drawn by what looked like a pair of goats. "Sir, I – thank you. That's more than I thought I'd get." Beside him, Solveig squeezed his hand.

Odin grinned at him. "You helped to save my people – I think I owe the both of you. Now be off! I've work to do." He snapped his fingers and Gunnar appeared with a whinny, nuzzling Solveig as they mounted him.

Thor stepped off of the Bifrost onto snow that was already melting into slush as the weather warmed. His footsteps caught Liam and Elena's attention and they walked to meet him, Liam's arm hanging from a makeshift sling.

"Your father..." Liam asked, and Thor smiled at him.

"Still kicking. The battle took some interesting turns."

They looked at him quizzically, but the Æsir shook his head. "The tale can wait. We should head to the cave – Kieth and Solveig are on their way."

Liam nodded, but Elena hesitated. "Are they alright?"

The god paused, obviously uncomfortable with the question. "They-they're fine. I'll let them tell you the story." Liam frowned, sensing that Thor was dodging something, but chose to keep silent. He felt the god's gratitude as Elena changed subjects.

"There's something I don't get – why wasn't I hurt from the blast?" she asked.

"We weren't sure that you wouldn't be," Thor replied, walking nonchalantly through the snow in full battle garb, his mail chinking as he moved. "But since only one of the Æsir or one of their relics could hurt Loki at that point, and since I wasn't fully in this realm at the time – well. Let's just say it was a lucky guess."

"He figured that if he directed the blow it would be on a different – plane, was the word you used?" Liam asked. At Thor's nod he continued. "We used the hammer just to make it seem like a mortal attack so Loki wouldn't be prepared. The lightning actually came from Thor himself."

The god smiled. "See, because it was from the plane I was on, and Loki's spirit was technically speaking on the same plane, I reasoned that something on a different plane – like you, for instance – wouldn't be affected. The blast knocked Loki out of your system, and from there he was just draining on your resources."

Elena blinked. "And you thought this up by yourself."

"Well, yes," Thor said, his grin in no way modest.

"You're insane, you know that?" Elena asked.

"That's what he said too," the god replied, glowering at Liam, who laughed.

"I'm just glad it worked," he said, pulling Elena into a one armed hug.

Together they entered the cave, finding the Bifrost already glowing as it waited for them. Thor held out a hand for his hammer. "I'll wait for you here," he said as Liam passed it over. He turned to stand guard as they thanked him before stepping onto the bridge.

Before them stood two figures straight from mythology; one a woman warrior with wings who was garbed all in steel – the other, a huge man clothed in fur and mail with a bear pelt for a cloak. It took the whinny of Gunnar behind the duo for them to recognize the pair as Kieth and Solveig, and Elena ran to the valkyr with a sob.

"It's alright," the woman soothed as she patted her on the back, obviously unsure of what to do. "I made my choice."

Kieth and Liam exchanged grim smiles, the latter pulling the big berserk into a hug. Both were blinking when they pulled back, and Elena fell upon Kieth a moment later.

"What happened?" Liam asked thickly.

Solveig clasped his arm. "This idiot went and got himself killed. I couldn't let him come up here alone."

Kieth laughed as Elena brushed away tears. "Leave out the part where I killed a dragon to save you, why don't you."

She blinked innocently at him. "No, dear. That was the idiot part."

"You killed Jormung – Jorman – the snake thing?" Liam asked, shocked. He felt Thor perk up inside his mind at the question.

Kieth grinned at him, clasping a hand over Solveig's mouth as she started to speak. "I sure did."

You're sure? the god asked. Liam passed on the question.

Kieth frowned as the valkyr nodded. "Fairly. I carved through the heart."

Solveig, could you show me where? Thor asked. *You should be allowed on Midgard.*

She looked at Kieth, who shooed the trio off. "Go on, I'll wait here. He sounds worried."

The group returned at Thor's insistence to where Kieth and Solveig had bested Jörmungandr, the god obviously agitated when they met him past the Bifrost. It took a moment for them to realize that they were in the right place, and they only did because of the pool of blood that covered the ground.

"Where did it go?" Solveig asked, her hand falling to Gram.

Thor uttered a low growl, pointing to the track that furrowed the ground. It was slick with the same black blood, and in the dim light they could see that it led to the river. "Returning to the water…I feared this."

"I thought Kieth said he killed it," Liam groaned.

"We thought he had," Solveig replied grimly. "If it lived through that…"

Elena suddenly gabbed Liam's elbow. He followed her pointing finger to the sky, where the great fiery crack was visibly growing smaller. Thor stared at it, his eyes distant. "The forces of Muspellheim are closing it," he said after a moment. "They've admitted defeat – we won!"

With an audible snap and a wave of hot air, the crack closed completely. Darkness fell, and Thor raised Mjolnir as Solveig drew Gram. Their surroundings were lit by the orange and blue light, and the four sighed in relief as they realized the danger had passed.

"I should call George," Elena said after a moment. Liam grabbed her phone from his pocket and tossed it to her, glad to find that it was charged – perhaps because his body had been a conduit to lightning several times.

She walked a short distance away, dialing the number as she went. There was silence for a moment, and then they heard her speak. "George? Yeah, we're fine. But you're never going to believe who's here…"

While they waited for a pickup, Thor sent them back to Kieth. They explained what they had found, and for a moment his eyes flashed red. Solveig laid her hand on his arm and he closed his eyes for a moment; they were normal when he looked up.

"We'll be ready if he tries anything," he promised.

There was silence between the four. "So…you can't come back to Earth at all?" Elena finally broached.

He shook his head. "I can't, but Solveig can."

110

The valkyr nodded. "I'll visit often. And don't worry – I rather think we can work out some visitation rights for you two."

After today, I don't think there's anything my father wouldn't grant you, Thor chimed in. They all laughed.

"Besides," Kieth added once they had sobered, "I think Asgard could use another blacksmith. Someone has to make sure we're ready for the next time."

"You think war will come again?" Liam asked.

The immortal duo nodded. "We'll keep watch here – and leave Midgard in your hands."

The four clasped hands in agreement.

They bid farewell shortly after and returned to find Tom and Thor chatting. The young man grinned and clasped hands with the pair, glad to see them safe. "Thor's been telling me quite the story," he said. "Sorry I couldn't get help from the Order."

"I'll be doing something about that…" the god said softly. "They were given their gifts for a reason – maybe it's time they were reminded of that. I'll speak with my father."

"Keep me updated, please," Tom requested. "There have been far too many relic bearers who haven't had things explained to them in the past few years. The Council is shirking its duties."

Thor nodded his agreement. "I shall. Warn George that my father would like a meeting, please." He tossed Mjolnir to Liam, who caught it one handed. "And you – hold onto that for me. I'll reclaim it later."

Liam nodded. 'Thank you for coming to help."

Elena hugged the god, her hair rising as she did so. "And for saving me," she added.

Thor blushed. "You would have done the same." With a final nod he was off. Liam felt a wall of exhaustion hit him as soon as the god was gone. "Owww…" he groaned as Tom and Elena caught him.

The butler cast a critical eye over his wrist. "Let's get you home – I'll patch you up there."

"Sounds good," the cop admitted. "I'm just gonna close my eyes…"

Friggsday

I enter the council late, my departure from Midgard somewhat hindered by my reluctance to leave. Saying goodbye to my new friends was harder than I would have thought, for all that I know I'll see them again.

The session is already begun as I enter Gladsheim and take my seat to the right of my father's own throne, if a little lower. He nods at me without halting his speech, continuing to tell the others of the events of the past week – both in Asgard and in Midgard.

The hall is packed, with many of the crowd spilling out into Idavale. Though normally such a council would be for the Æsir alone, today my father has chosen to spread the news of what has transpired to any who would hear it. Jötun mingle with the Æsir, and I am surprised at how accepting they are of one another.

My eyebrows continue to climb in surprise as I spot one of the Norns in the crowd, though I cannot tell which one. She cocks her head at me, and for a moment her eyes glow in a myriad of colors, shooting me a wink before they fade once more into the gray of her cowl.

Liam's voice comes to me suddenly. How's it going? *he asks, his strange accent still jarring in my mind. I feel his exhaustion, but for some reason he is here. I suspect my father has summoned him.*

Well enough, I suppose. For now he's just filling the others in, *I reply. My father's mouth twitches in a smile as he glances towards me, and I look down, hastily telling Liam to keep quiet until we're done.*

"In short," *my father finishes,* "The Ragnarök has been postponed by the acts of a few brave mortals and the aid of those we have long thought enemies. A truce is being drawn up with the Jötun as we speak. I do not know when the Time of the Doom will come again; nor, indeed, whether we shall survive it once more. We are in uncharted territory, my vision clouded by all of the possibilities before us. All that I know is that, should the Ragnarök come again, we will not stand alone."

Well said, *Liam murmurs, and I nod in agreement at my father's unusual eloquence.*

"And now, my friends, I must ask you to leave my son and I to our own council. We have much to discuss and to decide."

The crowd talks amongst themselves as they file out, some more slowly than others. The Norn remains behind, standing in the center of the room between all of the thrones. My mother is the last to leave, giving us a small smile before grabbing the handles of the doors. My father waits until the great carved doors are closed before addressing the Norn.

"Skuld," *he begins respectfully.* "We are honored by your presence."

"As I was honored by your invitation, king – though I confess to leaving before it arrived. I'm sure it is quite lovely." *Liam chuckles within my mind, an act which still seems unnatural to me, and she turns to him.* "Hello, Liam – and Thor. You've done well."

Thank you, lady, *he replies, his tone sincere, and I nod in satisfaction at his manners. She laughs, returning her gaze to my father.* "Now then, what would you have of me, All-father?"

"For now, simply to listen," *he answers.* "There are many things we must decide upon today, and I would have your council upon them."

She frowns "Know that there is little advice that I can freely give you – and understand this as well. You have said that your own vision is clouded by the future; I fear that mine is little better. Perhaps what paths are chosen today will clear the fog – and perhaps not. But I will listen."

He nods slowly, obviously troubled by her words, but turns to us. "Thor, my son – and Liam. Let me again thank you. You have done the impossible this past week, and showed great courage in doing so." *The human and I both begin to protest, but he raises his hand, silencing us. He waits a moment longer before continuing.* "I know that these events have been trying, and through them, you have forged a bond stronger than I could ever have imagined. This…could prove troublesome."

"Never before in our history have a mortal and an Æsir held such a close bond. Even those on Midgard who have possessed their relics for the longest have never been able to communicate so well as you two can. We gods have done our best these past centuries to remain removed from mortal affairs, and I fear this would prove difficult for Thor given your bond."

My father pauses for a moment, considering his words. "Liam, I would offer you a place in our halls and a seat in Valhalla, but I have a feeling you would refuse."

I can feel Liam nod as he speaks. Thank you for the offer – I'm honored. But I've my own duties here on Earth, and I won't shirk them.

"I'd imagine the girl has something to do with that as well," *I tease, and my father chuckles.*

Odin bows his head. "Speaking of Elena, thank her for the bravery she showed, would you?" *Liam nods, and my father continues.* "But she too has a choice. Please ask her when you awake what she wishes done with the sandals. We will honor whatever choice she makes." *Liam hesitates this time, but nods again.*

"Back to the two of you. Perhaps it would be for the better if Thor reclaimed Mjolnir." *Skuld stirs slightly, but says nothing.*

"No." *The word comes from both of us, and my father shakes his head, holding up a hand for us to let him finish.* "Mjolnir is needed here, in Asgard, to defend us – and I do not know what the consequences of your continued bond would be. Already you are closer than I would like."

I can feel Liam nudge me, and I hold my tongue to allow him to speak first. Sir, you may have sworn not to meddle in the affairs of mortals, and I can respect that. But your enemies have not, and we can't face them alone – and I think that sometimes you need help too. Thor and I can warn both sides of what's going on, and if something like this ever happens again... *he trails off.*

My father weighs his words carefully. "I understand your points," he says slowly. "But our borders are not as well protected as I would like, particularly after yesterday's battle. The Jötun will strengthen our defenses, but not all of them are friendly. Regardless, Thor is responsible for guarding the borders, and Mjolnir has always been at his side."

This time Liam lets me speak. "I've figured that out already, father." He looks at me in surprise. *"Yes, Mjolnir is needed, as am I – and you worry that our connection may be too strong. I confess, I would love to have my hammer back, but not all of it is needed to defend us."*

Liam grins widely as he catches on to my idea. "What if I were to leave Liam a part of Mjolnir's handle? It would not diminish its powers, and would leave Liam with enough of a connection to us to still make us an effective warning force."

"Likewise, it should serve to dull the connection between us somewhat, allowing us a little bit of peace in our own minds – though I suspect our bond will always be stronger than that of other relic bearers."

We quiet as we watch my father consider, and I reflect on how strange it is to think of Liam as a part of me. We've known each other for so little time, and yet the thought of being separated is almost painful to consider. My father eyes me, and I know he understands my thoughts.

"Very well," he says after a moment, his voice reluctant. "I can think of no better path, and this seems the best line of defense we can conspire. The hammer will be divided, if it will allow."

Skuld suddenly lets out a deep sigh, fog rolling from her sleeves and hood. She tilts her head back, though her bearing is not so dramatic as the first time Liam heard her utter a prophecy. Her voice grows deep, though it still sounds questioning, as though she herself does not fully understand the words she speaks.

They stand alone and tip the scale
Are any left to tell the tale?
For now there are, and hope remains
But doom will come, the gods' own bane
It comes once more, merely delayed
The trickster yet follows his fate
But not alone will Æsir stand
Mortals will join their hopeful band
A pact once made, never forgot
New bonds are forged and tales are taught
Remember now the myths of men

And all they have pushed past to win
Know that you do not stand alone
The day you hear the Doom Bell's tone.

Though the first lines of the poem are familiar, the rest rings new, and Liam and I both feel a shiver run up our spines at the sound of the words. The fact that it was uttered only after *the choice to share Mjolnir was made furthers our worry.*

Slowly Skuld returns to herself. When she speaks, her voice is unsure. "More than this, I cannot tell you. There is so much yet to be done...I must return to my sisters. Perhaps together we can make sense of what is even now being woven."

My father and I barely have time to raise our hands in farewell before she vanishes – there one minute and gone the next with no theatrics. Liam lets out a low whistle, my father nodding his slow agreement.

I thought they always knew what was going on? *Liam asks.*

I nod. "Anything powerful enough to block the eyes of a Norn is not something I would care to face. And it sounds like we aren't done with Loki yet."

Can we ever be rid of him? *Liam says with a groan.* But what is the Doom Bell?

My father shakes his head, his forehead creased with worry. "I cannot say. I have never heard of it before."

I know we use a similar phrase on earth when referring to someone whose time appears to be up, *Liam says slowly.* But somehow that doesn't seem to explain it.

We are silent for a moment. "Only time will tell, I think," *Odin says with a grimace.* "Though what the story shall be I am loathe to ask."

I feel Liam hesitate before he speaks – a trait that I did not know him to possess. His voice is soft as he asks, What of Kieth and Solveig?

My father looks at me, through me, to Liam, and I can see the pity in his eye. "They fought bravely – in both this realm and your own. They shall be rewarded for their actions, along with all of those who fought upon the plains of Vígríðr."

Liam nods quietly. But they'll remain here.

Odin's voice is soft. "Yes. They both made their choice, and not even the Æsir may refute what was done. That is left to a higher power. However, the Bifrost will always remain open to you and Elena. You may visit your friends as often as you wish."

I feel Liam's joy and laugh at it, but he ignores me.

Thank you, sir, *he tells my father, his words sincere.*

"No," *Odin replies.* "Thank you. Without you, we might not be speaking now."

And me, of course, *I send Liam's way.* You know I'm the real hero here.

He snickers, but gratitude tinges his words. Oh, certainly. I'm blessed to have such a noble friend.

Too right you are, *I reply, and my father laughs. It is good to see him smile – years slide off of his face as his eye sparkles, his cheeks rosy. I resolve to make him laugh more often, and feel Liam agree with me.*

Odin shakes his head. "Enough time for joking later. For now, sleep, and heal – for you have earned your rest." *He waves his hand, and I feel Liam fade in my mind as he drifts into slumber.*

"Come, my son," *the All-father beckons to me.* "We too deserve some sleep."

Just now, I couldn't agree with him more.

Liam awoke in a bed he didn't know, his arm stiff in a cast. Murmured conversation could be heard somewhere below him. Beside him, Elena dozed on a cot. On his other side was an end table, and upon it rested a small round disk, the inside an iridescent metal that looked familiar.

A small hole was bored through the disk, a gray leather string that brought to mind the Norns robes threaded through it. Liam sat up stiffly and slipped Mjolnir's pommel over his head, smiling as he felt Thor sleeping. Their connection was fainter than it had been, but still clear.

Elena sat up groggily. "How are you feeling?" she asked with a yawn.

"Stiff. Sore. *Hungry.*" he replied. "Want to bet Tom has food made?"

She laughed. "No bet!"

He grinned at her. "And you? How are you holding up?"

She paused for a moment, considering. "I honestly don't know – everything is still kind of a blur. I'm half convinced it was a dream."

Liam's chest tightened. "Do you remember anything?"

She looked at him, her eyes bright. "One thing is pretty clear, yeah. Did you mean it?"

He grinned at her. "What do you think?"

Elena shook her head, chuckling, and grabbed his collar. She pulled him in for a kiss, careful of his wrist, and for a while food was forgotten.

They stayed the rest of the day, having slept through most of it, but both agreed that they needed to get home by the next morning. They filled George in on the events of the battle, the old scholar taking notes all the while.

George told them that Odin had contacted him during the day, and after much discussion a meeting of the Order had been called. Odin had seemed furious at their inactivity and had promised to attend the meeting in person. George and Tom invited the duo, but they declined. "I think we've had enough adventures this week," Elena explained with a laugh.

Saturday

Time passes, and memory fades – sometimes more quickly than others. When Liam returned home from his week long odyssey, he found that his force had no memory of his departure, and that the time he had taken had been a paid vacation, requested weeks prior. Not a one of them even mentioned the full beard he now bore proudly, if trimmed somewhat from its former bushiness.

His dog, however, was thrilled to see him.

Elena likewise found that her family had expected her to be gone, though they weren't entirely sure where she had been. She truthfully told them that she had been staying with George, who sent his greetings to her father and promised to come and visit sometime.

Later that day the hospital staff where her father was having his therapy called, informing her that a generous sponsor had come forth and made a large donation to her father's cause – in fact, it would pay for all of his treatments. The only name the mysterious man left was High.

The news that day was full of the strange events of the past week – weather changes, increased wildfires, and some rather spectacular lightning storms. Liam was relieved to find a small spotlight on Kevin, the thief from the caves. He had been cleared of all charges, the police finding evidence that he really had been blackmailed into stealing the money by a man who had threatened his family – a man described as looking incredibly scruffy, with only one eye, long white hair, and leaning upon a staff carved with two ravens.

After a few days of deliberation and several video conferences with George, Elena chose to return the sandals. She and Liam agreed that though it would be good to keep an eye on Loki, there were better ways of doing so. The trickster had returned to his old prison, and when Solveig came to pick up the sandals she said she and Kieth would be setting up a guard to keep watch on him.

Later in the week Liam caught sight of his old neighbor leaving the house. "Mrs. Meyers!" he called. "I'm so sorry I wasn't here to help with your groceries last week, things came up-"

The old woman cut him off, shaking her head and patting his shoulder briskly. "It's quite alright, my dear lad. I know all about it." She winked at him, and Liam's brow furrowed as he wondered what strange rumors she might have heard.

She looked at him for a moment, her eyes shining with laughter, and then reached up slowly to tuck her hair behind her ear. The golden orb earring he had never seen her without shone in the restored sunlight, and she winked again before turning and shuffling off, leaning heavily upon her stroller.

Hey, that looks a lot like Freyja's necklace, Thor said suddenly. *I think my father has the Order keeping tabs on you!*

"No," Liam murmured, watching her shuffle slowly up her driveway. "No, no, no. No way. Not Mrs. Meyers."

The god laughed at him.

Someday

Elena walked past Old Maine, glad to be signed up for classes once more now that her father was on his way to recovery. Her old teachers had given written consent that she be allowed to take her final tests for the classes she had dropped out of and then proceed to her new courses, for which she was thankful.

She smiled as she saw Liam stand from a nearby bench, a flower held sheepishly in his hand. "Hi there," he said, offering it to her.

"Hello," she replied shyly, taking it from him. This whole dating thing was new to her, but if he kept being this sweet she wasn't sure she minded – even if it wasn't exactly a normal courtship. "Hear anything from Thor?"

He grinned as she broke the ice and they began to walk towards the parking lot, Liam taking her hand in his as they did so. It felt natural, their strides changing to match one another. "Nothing much, just an occasional snippet. I can still feel him, but we're not talking all the time."

He rubbed one hand through his bushy beard, still trying to get used to the feeling, and Elena laughed at him. She stood on tiptoe to kiss his cheek, the bristly hairs of his beard tickling her nose as she did so. He blushed. "I like it," she said.

"Good," Liam replied. "Cause it's growing on me."

Thor gave him a mental backhand for the pun as the two walked off, all prophecies put aside – for now.

And in the darkness, something stirred – and laughed…

The relic-bearers will return in

Chosen of the Gods
Lovesick

Author's Note

My elementary school library had a book on Norse mythology that I loved. I'm pretty sure I kept that book on constant check-out until I had all of the stories memorized. One of my first memories of my school life is of encouraging my friends to check out the book once I had (finally) turned it in. I wanted to show them how amazing the Norse myths could be.

It has been my experience that most of North America is more familiar with the Greek gods and goddesses than they are with the Norse. While I love the Greek myths, my heart belonged first to Norse mythology. I wrote Hammerfall because I wanted to share my love of that mythology with anyone who would read it. I guess you could say that this story was written for the same reason I wanted my elementary school friends to check out the book – so that they could experience the same joy that I had found within the stories.

I hope that Hammerfall was able to share a little bit of that joy with you. I hope it made you curious, made you want to know more about the stories mentioned within. Above all else, I hope it took you to another world, even if only for a short time.

Thank you for letting me share that world with you.

Until next book,

Natasha Cover